This book is on loan from
Library Services for Schools
www.cumbria.gov.uk/
libraries/schoolslibserv

County Council

INTO THE VOLCANO

JESS BUTTERWORTH

Orion

ORION CHILDREN'S BOOKS

First published in Great Britain in 2021
by Hodder and Stoughton

1 3 5 7 9 10 8 6 4 2

A CIP catalogue record for this book
is available from the British Library.

ISBN 978 1 51010 851 6

Typeset in Mrs Eaves by
Palimpsest Book Production Ltd, Falkirk, Stirlingshire

Printed and bound in Great Britain by Clays Ltd, Elcograf S.p.A.

The paper and board used in this book are made
from wood from responsible sources.

Orion Children's Books
An imprint of
Hachette Children's Group
Part of Hodder and Stoughton
Carmelite House
50 Victoria Embankment
London EC4Y 0DZ

An Hachette UK Company

www.hachette.co.uk
www.hachettechildrens.co.uk

To Jonathan

Seb

Red Rocks, Colorado, USA

24th June, 8 a.m.

♥ THE TEN OF HEARTS ♥

My favourite card is the ten of hearts. I like the pattern those ten hearts make on the face of the card. Sometimes I trace the design with my thumb, finding different ways to connect each shape, the card smooth and silky under my skin. Today, I rub the circle of hearts in the middle.

There's a 1-in-52 chance that I'll pick the ten of hearts straight from a normal deck of cards the first try. So far, it's only happened once, and I've tried *waaaay* over fifty-two times. With my special deck of all hearts it happens more often, but it's not as satisfying.

I place the ten of hearts back in my special deck and tap my feet against the frayed edges of the vinyl seat in front of me. I've been waiting for this trip to Dinosaur Ridge for weeks. Everyone on the bus is chattering away. Next to me, Clay's head is buried in his *Calamity Stoppers* notebook. We created the game together. I read the rules, neatly printed in Clay's handwriting, on the back.

THE GAME: CALAMITY STOPPERS

A role-playing, group storytelling game for four players and a Game Master

Strange things have started happening. An evil entity named Calamity is travelling around the world, causing chaos. It has released invading plant and animal species, polluted rivers and seas and knocked down buildings and wonders of the world.

Your job is to find and capture Calamity before the world is COMPLETELY DESTROYED.

You will need:
Up to five decks of cards (one for each player and one for the Game Master)

How to play:
1. Create your character. Pick a card. The suit is your superpower. Every player must have a different suit.

Clubs: You have super strength. You can lift, move or destroy any object.

Hearts: You have telepathy/mind control. You can persuade people, read their true intentions and discover truth.

Spades: You can transform into an animal. You can choose any animal but you must wait three rounds before each change.

Diamonds: You are indestructible. You will never feel pain or be damaged. You can shield other team members.

2. Create your deck by combining all the cards of your suit from each player's deck. Your deck is then made only of your suit. E.g. If your superpower is clubs, your deck will be made up of only clubs.

3. Create the story. The Game Master reads the book and leads the story. You imagine what your character would do throughout the story and suggest their actions out loud.

4. Determine the outcome of your character's actions. For every action you

> want your character to do, you pick a
> card to determine how successful that
> action will be. High card = high success.
> Low card = low success. A King is a
> critical success, an ace is a critical
> failure. The Game Master has the final
> say and narrates the story. For example,
> if the club character player wanted to
> lift up a car off the ground and they
> picked a two of clubs, the Game Master
> might say, 'You go to lift up the car but
> the bumper is covered in oil and you just
> can't get a good grip on it.' Once you've
> used your cards you have to rest by
> missing a turn before reshuffling the pack.

'Not prepared for the campaign on Friday?' I
ask Clay, teasing him.

He looks up, shocked. His blonde hair falls
across his face and he shakes it off his eyes. 'I'm
totally prepared. These are just the finishing
touches.'

I laugh. Clay takes his position as Game Master
very seriously. The handbook is covered in scrawls
from his notes. We created the game together
last year and play with Ava, Emily and Zac but
to be honest, Clay's done most of the work.

'It *is* the finale,' he says. His eyes light up. 'I'm allowed to make it awesome. Just you wait until you see where we're going to end up.'

Clay's story has taken us from battling locust swarms at the pyramids in Egypt to rescuing dolphins in the Amazon, as each of our characters tries to save the world, while Clay, the Game Master, throws obstacles in our way. Wolfie is his alias as the narrator.

'The bottom of the ocean?' I suggest.

He smirks and shakes his head. 'It's somewhere we've always wanted to go.'

I squint, thinking hard. 'I dunno. New Zealand?'

'Guess again,' he replies.

'Oh, come on. Tell me,' I say, trying to peer at his sketches.

'No way. You've got to wait.' Clay shuts the handbook firmly.

I roll my eyes at him then stare out the window. The skies are clear and blue. The roads are busy, filled with campers and RVs. Everyone seems to be heading up to the mountains to enjoy the beautiful weather.

We're almost at Dinosaur Ridge. The green, tree-filled slopes around us are becoming bare. I keep my eyes peeled for layers of red and orange rock in the mountainside. We learnt they're the perfect place to find dinosaur fossils and tracks.

When the Rocky Mountains formed, the older, harder layers of rock from when the dinosaurs lived were tilted and forced up. The softer, newer layers that were on top have since eroded, leading to all these awesome dinosaur discoveries.

'What do you call a sleeping dinosaur?' I ask Clay.

He shrugs.

'A dino-*snore*,' I say.

'That is *not* funny,' says Clay, but he can't stop himself from laughing and then I get the giggles.

'Can you bring the noise level down a bit please, Seb?' asks Mr Evans, standing up and looming in the narrow passage between the seats. He's wearing a university sweatshirt. It's weird seeing him not dressed in his usual tie and suit.

'Yes, Mr Evans,' I say, before ducking behind the seat in front and doing an impression of him.

'Stop it,' whispers Clay, even though he's smiling. Mr Evans is a good teacher but can be strict.

I've always been loud. When I was younger I went to speech therapy to try and learn how to talk quieter but it turned out I just have a loud voice. I can't pretend I don't. One good thing about it is that everyone wants me to be in their group in choir and debate. The downside is that I can't get away with talking to Clay or any of my other friends in class, even if I whisper. Sometimes I even get blamed for other people talking. Teachers just assume it's me!

The first time Mr Evans told me to be quiet at the beginning of this school year, I replied, 'BUT THIS IS MY NORMAL VOICE.' And everyone laughed, even though I was only being honest. Now it's become a whole inside joke with my friends that we all say whenever anyone is told to be quiet.

The seats shudder as the road gets steeper. In front, Maddison and Brooke are misting up the windows and drawing pictures on them.

'Has everyone finished their quizzes?' asks Mr Evans.

A few people shout yes, followed by some mumbles of no.

'You have two more minutes,' says Mr Evans.

'What'd you get?' Clay asks me.

I read out my result: 'If you answered mostly As you're a Struthiomimus! You're fast, have long legs, a tail and a toothless beak! Your name means "ostrich mimic" because you resemble an ostrich. You're medium-sized. What about you?' I ask.

'If you answered mainly Cs you're a Cryolophosaurus! You're a large meat-eater, with a crest on your head. You live in Antarctica.'

'The dinosaurs you've been assigned are the

ones you're going to be doing your research projects on,' says Mr Evans from the front.

The bus fills with groans.

'I wanted to be a Diplodocus,' I whisper to Clay. 'That's my favourite one.'

'I wanted to be a Pterodactyl,' he replies.

'That's not a dinosaur,' I say, shaking my head.

'Yes it is,' says Clay, looking confused.

'I'm telling you, Pterodactyls aren't dinosaurs. They lived at the same time dinosaurs did, but they were flying reptiles.'

'Well, I think you're wrong. We'll find out when we get there!' Clay crosses his arms.

Clay and I are both stubborn. That means we disagree all the time, but we've still been best friends for ever. Nothing will ever change that.

The bus slows, pulls into a busy gas station and rolls to a stop behind a line of cars. It's a big gas station, but it's packed so we have to wait to get a place. When we finally pull forward, the bus takes up two spaces. Behind the pumps, there's a large square building with a red stripe painted along it. Across the windows is written: Cold drinks. Snacks. Candy.

Mr Evans stands up at the front of the bus and checks his watch.

'We're stopping for ten minutes. Use the restroom. Buy a snack if you want. But I want everyone back on this bus by eight thirty. Got it?'

'Yes, Mr Evans,' we all respond.

'I'm thirsty,' says Clay. 'Let's go in.'

Inside it's air-conditioned. It smells of fries and burgers. A 90s song Mom loves, but I can't remember the name of, blares out over the speakers. At one end is a fast food counter, at the other is a check-out register.

There are about forty people inside. Most are gathered around the fast food. I try on some funny star-shaped shades, then grab a bag of chips and head towards the fridges at the back.

I wait patiently for an older lady with a pink scarf tied around her head to get her drink.

She touches a can, scoffs, then puts it back and reaches into the fridge, her head almost disappearing inside. She stands on tippy-toes.

'Can I help you?' I ask.

'Oh, you are a dear,' she says, pulling her head back out. She's wearing oval shades and her white hair is swept elegantly back under her scarf. She's dressed in a matching green blouse and shorts and looks pretty stylish for an old lady. 'Can you reach one of the lemonades at the back? The ones at the front are still warm.'

I smile. My grandma would have been determined to get the coldest lemonade too. I'm a bit taller than she is, so I can just reach one of the cold, back-of-the-fridge cans. 'Here you go,' I say, handing it to her.

'Thank you, darling. Have a good day.' She waves before turning towards the aisle filled with cookies, chips and dried fruit and nuts.

'You too!' I say.

I'm just in time to join Clay at the front of the line to pay, skipping the six people waiting behind him. There's a young guy with long hair at the counter.

'I'm gonna use the restroom,' says Clay, after we've paid. 'I'll meet you back on the bus. Don't let them leave without me,' he adds jokingly.

On my way out, I hold the door open for a man in a hoodie with his hands in pockets. His light skin is peeling from sunburn and beads of sweat stick to the flakes. I pass him. Why is he wearing a hoodie? It's boiling even in the air conditioning.

Back on the bus, I open the chips and munch on them. Mr Evans starts the register.

'Clay's not back yet,' I say, when it comes to his name.

Then there's a bang. Everyone looks up and hushes.

It's as loud as a firework. I search the sky for a rogue rocket. It's still clear and cloudless.

I look to Mr Evans for reassurance but his brow is creasing with worry.

'What was that?' asks Maddison.

The bang sounds again. And again.

It's coming from inside the gas station.

And that's when I realise what it is.

Gunshots.

Vivi

London, UK
24th June, 3 p.m.

I pull my hood up as I run for the bus. Although it's supposed to be the start of summer, it's drizzling and grey. Butterflies churn in my stomach. This is it. The most important moment of my life — I've been working towards this for years — and I'm going to be late!

I repeat my audition lines in my head. Earlier, during tutorial, Ms Peters had caught me looking them up on my phone. She had marched over, her beady, magpie-like eyes gleaming, and confiscated my phone.

'You can get it back after detention on Monday,' she'd said with a satisfied nod as she shoved it in her pocket.

'But today's only Thursday!' I'd replied, my breathing panicky. Dad would be upset. He likes to have the option of texting me when I'm at Mum's. 'I need it over the weekend.'

'You can do detention tonight instead if you really want to,' Ms Peters had suggested.

Two choices. Risk missing my audition or have no phone over the weekend.

Great. Each was as rubbish as the other.

I'd thought fast. The weekend would be tricky without a phone. When Mum and Dad divorced, I'd said I wanted to live with Dad. There was no way I was going to move in with Mum and Mr McBoring — not when I would have had to change school too. So now I go to Mum's at the weekend and use my phone to keep in touch and organise pickup with Dad.

On the other hand, I couldn't risk missing this audition. It could change everything. But if I rushed there straight from detention, I could still make it . . .

In the end I'd decided to get my phone back and go to detention. But right now, as I dodge a teacher with an umbrella and leap over a puddle, I wish I'd chosen a weekend without my phone. By the time I get on the bus I'm hot and sweaty and my hair's gone frizzy from the rain. *Perfect*. Exactly the audition look I was going for. Not.

I try to smooth my hair down with my fingers. It feels static, like I've been rubbing it with a balloon.

I should have known better than to try and fit a detention in before my audition, especially with Dad not being able to drive me because of his work meeting.

A honk from outside brings me out of my thoughts. We're only one stop away from the theatre now but the bus is stuck in traffic. I glance at the time on my phone. Ten minutes until I'm supposed to be there. Of all the things to mess up. Grandma Mimi said that if I get this part, then she'll fly over from the States to see me in the play. I've had the lead in school plays before, but this production is with the British Youth Theatre and I'd be performing in my favourite professional theatre over the summer holidays. And Rita Ali, the famous director, will be working with us! She's directed plays on the West End *and* Broadway.

Finally, painfully slowly, the bus edges to the next stop and the driver opens the doors.

'Thanks!' I yell as I jump off and dash into the theatre. I push open the door and arrive, breathless. The theatre has that old building smell, wood with a hint of cold and damp. My shoes track mud onto the new red carpets they put in this year.

A lady in a theatre group logo t-shirt, holding a clipboard, waits by the box office and smiles as I approach. Putting on my most professional tone, I say, 'Vivi Berry, auditioning for the role of Alice.'

'You're just in time,' she replies. 'Do you have your permission slip?' I hand her the form that Mum and Dad signed saying that I could audition for the part. She ticks me off the list and leads me along a passage with ornate carvings on the walls, into the wings. 'Break a leg,' she whispers.

'Thanks!' I reply, my voice quavering.

This stage will be the biggest I've ever been on. Will my voice fill the space? Will anyone hear me? Nerves gather in my stomach. I stand in the darkness of the wings and wait for them to call my name, biting the skin around my nail.

When I'm acting, I lose myself in an imaginary world, just like I used to when I was little and playing make-believe. I forget everything going on in my own life, because nothing happening off the stage matters. When it goes well, I feel like anything is possible.

Today, I don't have time to do my whole warm-up routine. All I can do is my breathing exercises, the ones I do before every audition. It calms my inner voice.

What if they don't think you're any good?

My earliest memory is my aunt telling me I was 'born for the stage', just like my grandma. I've heard it lots since then.

Vivi's got her grandma's talent.

Vivi's so talented.

Vivi's following in her grandma's footsteps.

Grandma's an opera singer *and* an actor. She's toured all over the world. I spoke to her about the audition last night. '*I* believe in you one hundred per cent. They'd be fools not to cast you!' she'd said.

Which, if I'm being honest, made me feel *extra* nervous.

My breathing isn't doing much to calm my inner monologue today. I close my eyes and focus, trying to meditate. It's what my drama teacher tells us to do.

'Vivi Berry?'

I open my eyes, plant a huge smile on my face, put my shoulders back and walk out in front of the casting directors.

'Hi!' I say, after I've made it to the centre of the stage. I blink, my eyes adjusting to the bright lights. Rows and rows of red seats stretch out before me. I've never been on an actual professional theatre stage before. Memories flash through my mind — watching *Billy Elliot* here with Mum, all the plays Grandma brought me to whenever she came to visit: *Matilda*, *Romeo and Juliet*, *Annie*. I picture where we were sitting, sometimes in the upper circle, sometimes closer to the front in the grand circle. I remember the excited buzz of the audience, the hush as the music faded and the blackout before the plays had begun.

'Hi, Vivi,' says one of the casting directors. There's four in total, all sitting in the front row, clutching pens. One has a big smile. Her hair is frizzy like mine. The others look serious and tired.

'You're here to audition for the part of Alice?' the smiling one asks.

'Yes,' I say.

'Great. Whenever you're ready,' she replies.

I nod and step back. I take a deep breath and

melt into the part, acting as if I'm tumbling down a very long hole.

'I wonder how many miles I've fallen by this time?' I say, staring around me. 'I must be getting somewhere near the centre of the earth. Let me see: that would be four thousand miles down, I think.'

I look out over the casting directors, as if I'm pondering. They're smiling and nodding at me. As I turn away again, I notice one of them is wearing a pink scarf. It looks just like the scarf that Grandma always wears, the one she calls her 'signature scarf'. She ties it around her head and wears it along with big dangly earrings that make her ears stretch.

I picture the delight and pride on Grandma's face if she got to watch me here playing Alice one day.

It's enough to pull me from the part. I'm not immersed in the world any more. My inner voice comes flooding back.

What if I forget my lines?

And then, I do. My mind goes completely blank. I shake my head. I'm out of character now.

'Um,' I stutter.

My heart pounds in my ears. *What's the stupid line?* I rub my face with my hands.

I glance out over the casting directors. Three

are frowning, but the one in the scarf appears concerned. I look away, not wanting to see her concern turn to disappointment. Out of the corner of my eye, the pink scarf ripples as if there's a breeze.

Seb

Red Rocks, Colorado
24th June, 8.40 a.m.

♠ THE ACE OF SPADES ♠

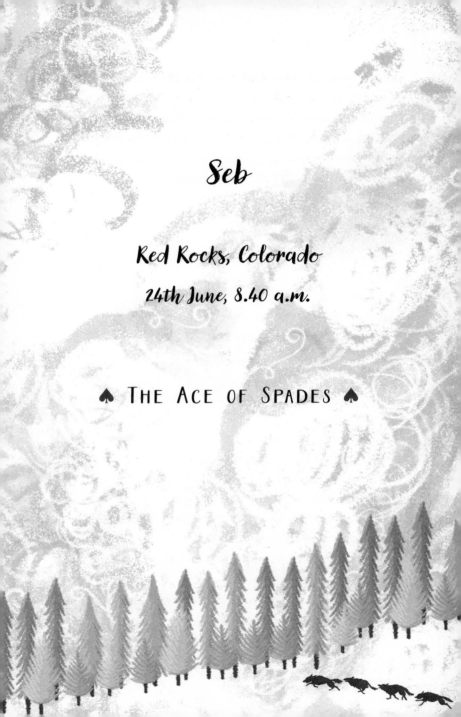

We've practised what to do if there's ever a shooter in school.

I know what to do if I'm in a classroom or a corridor. The teacher will lock the door and we'll hide behind a display or under a table, away from windows or the door.

But I don't know what to do on a bus.

We've never practised on a bus.

There's another bang.

A split second of silence follows.

Then screams fill the air.

'Everyone down!' yells Mr Evans. He helps Mo and Esme get onto the floor.

The gas station door opens and people run out. I look and I don't see Clay.

'Seb, get down,' shouts Mr Evans.

I slip off the seat and crouch on the cold metal floor, cramped.

Clay's still inside.

Who's going to protect Clay?

There's another shot.

I duck down, sheltering under the benches. Chewing gum covers the underside of the seat in front in rainbow colours.

I hear one of the panels of glass in the shop window smash.

The bus is hot and smells of plastic. My stomach heaves. I feel sick.

'Can bullets go through a bus?' asks Brooke in a scared whisper.

On the floor under the seats is a collection of trampled objects: an empty chip bag, a purple leaflet, a lone ace of spades.

'Why aren't we driving to safety?' asks Maddison urgently. 'We need to go!'

'Clay's still inside,' I say, my voice cracking. *I have to do something.*

I begin to stand, peer out of the window. I can see people running in all directions, but I can't find Clay.

Mr Evans crawls along the non-slip carpet down the aisle towards me. 'Seb, look at me,' he says, pulling my shoulders away from the window and back down towards the floor. 'It's going to be OK.'

I let my body sink down and turn to look at him. His eyes are filled with sadness and worry.

And I wish that I could believe him.

Vivi

London
24th June, 3.41 p.m.

I stare up at the bright stage lights and blink. I try and remember the lines. Any of them. Even the one I just said. But adrenaline courses through my body and my mind remains blank.

'I'm sorry,' I stammer. 'I don't know what happened.'

'Would you like to start again?' offers one of the directors.

I clear my throat but can't bring myself to speak.

'*I wonder how many miles I've fallen by this time?*' she prompts me.

I repeat the line, but then stammer when I try to go on to the next. My cheeks burn. All I want is to get far, far away.

'Are you all right, dear?' asks the one in the scarf.

'I don't feel so good,' I say, which is true, although it's not the reason I'm failing. I don't know *why* I'm failing.

The directors glance at one another.

I find myself staring at the pink scarf again. I drag my eyes away and feel almost as if I'm floating.

I bite my lip to hold back tears, bow my head and run offstage.

Luckily, there's no one outside waiting for me.

And just like that, it's over. My weeks of

planning and practising and rehearsing are gone in a second.

On the bus on the way home, I lean my head against the window and watch the buildings pass in a blur. Pigeons are gathered around the park gates next to an overflowing bin. It was supposed to be so different. Why did that have to happen *then*? It's never happened before. Not only have I blown my chance but I've completely embarrassed myself in front of the casting directors. *Brilliant.*

My breath is still coming fast. We pass a takeaway and the smell of Indian food fills the air. Dad will no doubt have made me pizza to celebrate. He always does.

What am I going to tell him?

Hi Dad. Today I got detention. And I didn't make it through the first round of the auditions.

I still can't believe what happened. We pass an ice-cream van playing Greensleeves.

My phone vibrates. Two missed calls from Dad. He's ringing to find out how the audition went. I can't face talking to him right now. I send him a quick text to let him know that I'm OK.

On the bus home. Can't ring. Low battery.

Dad always wants me to save my battery for emergencies.

I lean my head against the window. This

morning I thought today was going to be the best day ever but now it feels like the worst. My thoughts drift to Grandma. I hope she'll still visit soon even though I'm not in the play.

Seb

Red Rocks, Colorado
24th June, 8.42 a.m.

♥ THE QUEEN OF HEARTS ♥

I count twelve shots. I flinch each time. With each one, the sound cuts deeper and deeper into me.

And then, nothing.

In playing cards, the number twelve is represented by the queen.

'Is it over?' asks Brooke. Maddison cries gently next to her.

'Everyone stay down,' says Mr Evans. 'The police are on their way.'

I can hear the sound of sirens. 'Can you see Clay?' I ask Mr Evans.

'I think we should go!' yells Brooke.

'We can't leave without Clay!' I say.

Sirens grow louder. The police arrive in a blur of red and blue lights.

I lift my head and stand to look out. Behind them, I spot ambulances, screaming into the gas station. Someone's hurt. *What if it's Clay?*

'Stay down, Seb!' shouts Mr Evans.

I'm forced to wait, sitting on the floor, with no idea what's happening outside. Clay's backpack is still on his seat. The handbook sticks out the top of it. A piece of stuffing pokes out the side of my seat cushion and I pull at it, breaking it into little pieces.

Please, let no one be seriously hurt. Please, let Clay be OK.

I crouch down low.

Time passes. It feels like for ever. I can hear

shouting and running. And then I see Mr Evans stand up. Two police officers board the bus.

'The area has been secured. Everyone here OK?' one calls. None of us say anything, but Mr Evans speaks quietly to him and then he follows them off the bus.

A moment later, Mr Evans rushes back on and grabs Clay's backpack from next to me. I can hear sirens retreating into the distance now.

'Where's Clay?' I ask. 'Where are you going?'

But he's already hurried off the bus.

Ms Miller stands at the front of the bus. 'You can all sit down now,' she says. 'It's safe.'

Everyone rushes to look out of the window at the gas station.

'Stay in your seats!' says Ms Miller. 'Now, listen, everyone. The police are going to escort us back to school where your parents will meet us. The police may want to talk to some of you.' She pauses. 'Clay has been hurt and they're taking him to the hospital.' Her skin is pale and her usual sing-song voice comes out monotone.

I jump up. 'Was he shot?'

'Mr Evans is going to stay with him until his parents arrive,' she says, ignoring my question. 'He's going to be looked after really well and I'm sure everything will be OK.'

'I need to go with him too,' I say. 'He'll want me there.'

'I'm sorry, Seb,' she says gently. 'He's in the best hands.'

The bus is already pulling away from the pump. The police escort leads the way, siren lights flashing. I press my face up against the glass, ignoring the empty Clay-sized space next to me.

Vivi

London
24th June, 5.30 p.m.

The bus takes ages to get home. I expect the smell of pizza dough to hit me when I walk in, but there's nothing coming from the kitchen. In fact, the flat is eerily quiet.

'Dad?' I call. Dad's always home by now, even after a meeting. Plus, the front door was unlocked.

I walk along the corridor past the sitting room, the kitchen, and peer out to the garden. All empty. To the left, there's a rustling coming from Dad's bedroom.

'Dad?' I ask again as I push the door.

The first thing I see is an open suitcase on the floor.

'What's going on?' I ask.

'Vivi!' Dad rushes forward and hugs me. His stubbly cheeks smell faintly of sandalwood and pepper. His arms stay wrapped around me for longer than usual.

'Thank God you're home,' he whispers, holding me close.

'Is everything OK?' I ask, but I can tell it's not.

He lifts his head back, pushes back his long brown hair, and stares at me with deep-blue eyes. There are specks of brown in them too. The corners are red.

Has Dad been crying?

'Something's happened,' he says.

'What?' I ask. My chest tingles. 'What is it?'

He takes my hand and guides me to the bed with trembling fingers.

I sit down next to him and swallow. I'm not sure I want to hear what he's about to say.

He rubs his hand across his forehead. 'There was a shooting in America.'

Someone we know has been hurt. I can tell from the sorrow in his voice. I list the people it could be in my head.

My cousins.

My aunts and uncles.

'It's Grandma,' he says.

There's a knot in my stomach.

He looks up and meets my eyes. His glisten with tears.

'She died. I'm so sorry, sweetie.' He hugs me again.

I hear what he's just said, but the meaning doesn't register. All I can think about is Grandma, wearing her pink scarf, gesturing wildly as she tells a story, encouraging me about my acting, singing loudly as she drives. She *has* to be alive. I only spoke to her yesterday.

But as I look at Dad, I know he's telling the truth. Grandma is gone.

Seb

Denver, Colorado
25th June, 9 a.m.

♥ THE KING OF HEARTS ♥

The press is calling the incident a 'robbery gone wrong'. The shooter surrendered at the scene.

I don't know exactly what happened.

I do know that seven people were killed.

Clay is alive. But he's seriously hurt. He was shot and the bullet is *still* inside of him, close to his heart.

I'm waiting for Mom to get off the phone with Clay's dad. So far Mom has just nodded and said 'I can't imagine' and 'How awful' a bunch, as she runs her hands through her dark indigo hair.

She paces the kitchen. 'I mean it,' she says. 'Anything we can do to help just let me know.'

'What did he say?' I ask urgently as she hangs up.

She pours us both a glass of water and sits down at the table next to me.

'Clay is stable but critical,' she says.

The words swim around my head.

'That means he's not getting any worse at the moment, but they need to operate as soon as possible,' Mom continues. 'They're waiting for a specialist. It's a tricky operation.'

I nod. Surgery near the heart sounds dangerous.

'Ninety-five per cent of patients with gunshot wounds who get to the hospital with beating hearts survive,' Mom says. It sounds like she's repeating something she read online.

I know it's supposed to make me feel better. But that means there's a one-in-twenty chance Clay *won't* survive.

'He was behind a metal sign,' Mom goes on. 'That slowed the bullet down too. I'm sure he'll be all right, honey.'

I shake my head. That's got to improve Clay's chances a bit but it's not enough. If only I could improve them even more. I need him to *one hundred per cent* be OK. Mom rubs my back. My body feels stiff and tense.

'Can I go see him?' I ask, my voice quieter than usual.

She tilts her head to the side sympathetically. 'Only Clay's family are allowed to visit for now,' she says. 'We have to wait till he's a bit better.'

I can't believe the last proper conversation we had was an argument over whether Pterodactyls were dinosaurs.

'I thought I'd drop some food round for them,' Mom says. 'Would you like to come with me?'

I nod. All I want to do is see Clay. But at least going to his house is better than doing nothing.

Mom's made a casserole. We walk it over. Clay's dad is there when we arrive. 'I came to get clothes and things and then I'm going straight back to the hospital,' he says, gazing around. He looks lost in his own home. 'There's no more news.'

'Can I do anything to help?' I ask.

'Not right now,' says Clay's dad. He tries to smile, but his lip wobbles.

'Go put this in the fridge,' says Mom, passing me the casserole dish.

Clay's house is basically my second home. When everything with my dad happened, I stayed with him and his family for a few days. Clay and I built a fort and we played video games inside it while his dad made us grilled cheese sandwiches and cookies with milk. I didn't feel like leaving the fort so we ate everything inside.

But it feels weird to be here without Clay. The fridge is already full of pies and homemade food in ceramic dishes that neighbours have brought. I stack ours on top of another one. I leave Mom and Clay's dad talking in the entryway and wander upstairs into Clay's room. His bed is unmade and clothes are scattered across it. On the bed is his backpack, the game handbook sticking out.

I glance behind me, knowing I'm doing something I'm not supposed to, and slide the handbook out from the backpack.

Clay would be upset if he found out I was looking ahead in the game.

But we were meant to play the finale tonight.

And it's a little piece of him I can carry with me while he's in hospital.

I find the last page and smile. He's drawn a

map leading to a pool in Yellowstone National Park, labelled the Rainbow Pool. The words written underneath say:

Here, one wish will come true IF you follow the rules. They are:

1. At least two people must make the same wish together.
2. The adventuring party has to agree on what the wish will be.
3. You can't wish to destroy anything or anyone.

We'd completed a project about Yellowstone Park last semester in school and Clay was obsessed with the idea of going in real life. He wanted to see the wild animals, especially the wolves. I wanted to go to see the geology, the Earth itself.

I know that sounds boring, but Yellowstone is home to the largest caldera in the world. A caldera is an enormous crater formed by major volcanic eruptions millions of years ago. I wanted to see the spot where something so major had happened, something *so* big, that the evidence of it was still around thousands and thousands of years after it had happened.

And, even cooler, the caldera at Yellowstone is still an active supervolcano — although the last lava flow was seventy thousand years ago, so the chances of another eruption any time soon are pretty tiny. But there *are* currently geysers all over Yellowstone, which are hot springs that erupt with water.

What would we have wished for in the game? Probably for Calamity's location or something like that. So far, we've always been one step behind, clearing up the damage Calamity has created.

I flop down onto Clay's bed and hug the handbook to my chest, closing my eyes. If only our game and the wishes were real, and I really could make Clay better by finding that rainbow pool.

If only . . .

I glance down at the map.

Clay bases so many of our quests on real life, and I know he did a TON of research for this one. What if it *is* real? When Mr Evans was teaching us about it, he kept saying Yellowstone was a 'magical place'. What if there really is magic in the volcano? Maybe all us players could go there and make the wish, like Clay wanted us to?

Once I have the idea, I can't get it out of my head. It grows. I can feel it happening now.

And, for the first time since the incident, I feel like I can breathe.

I trace the rainbow pool with my fingers before digging my pack of cards out of my pocket. My superpower is telepathy, which means my whole pack is made of hearts. I shuffle them.

'I'm going to save Clay by wishing in the rainbow pool,' I say out loud. I turn over the top card. My stomach fills with butterflies. It's the king of hearts. The strongest card there is. A CRITICAL SUCCESS!

I know what I have do. Downstairs, Mom and Clay's dad are still talking. I grab my phone and call Ava, Emily and Zac on a group chat.

They all answer immediately.

'Any news?' asks Ava.

I update them that Clay's still in hospital, waiting for his operation.

Emily sighs.

'There might be something we can do to help,' I say quietly. They listen while I explain about the rainbow pool and the wish. 'We can go there and finish the game in real life!'

'Er, what do you mean?' asks Emily.

'I think the rainbow pool is a pool that really exists in Yellowstone,' I reply. 'And it's only twelve hours from here. We can find it. I think — I think it would help Clay get better, if we did.'

There's a long silence.

'There's no way that my mom will let me go,' says Zac finally. His voice is sad and apologetic.

'Yeah, mine neither,' says Ava.

'My parents basically won't let me out of their sight now,' Emily adds. 'I could try, but . . .' She trails off.

'Sorry, Seb,' says Ava. 'I really am. I wish there was something we could do.'

I sigh and say goodbye, ending the chat. I remember our last game here together, laughing and eating fries while we played in Clay's dining room. I know they like the game, but none of them are as serious as Clay and I are about it. We came up with the initial idea, we understand it the most.

'Seb!' Mom calls up the stairs. 'Time to go.'

I panic and stuff the handbook in my backpack. It's not technically stealing, I think. Just borrowing.

When I'm trying to make a decision, Mom always says I should do the thing that my future self will thank me for. I imagine my future self will be unhappy if Clay was in the hospital and I just sat around and did nothing. And the cards have spoken. Even if no one else from our game believes me, I need do everything I can.

And that means going to Yellowstone. Now I just need someone else to come and make the wish with me . . .

Vivi

London
25th June, 6 p.m.

Usually I love packing for trips. I lay out all my favourite clothes, like my baggy jeans and cropped shirts, and work out the perfect combination of items to take so I have different outfits for every day.

I love clothes. And I found some of my best clothes with Grandma. She'd always take me to thrift stores and she had a knack for spotting the most *amazing* vintage clothes in great condition.

But today I just stand and flick through my wardrobe, wondering what Grandma would want me to wear to her funeral. She always wore such brightly coloured outfits that I don't think she'd approve of me wearing black. I stop at a dark grey dress with pink flowers on it. It reminds me of Grandma's pink scarf. I roll it up and stuff it into my suitcase.

Grandma and Grandad moved to the States after Grandma had her first big singing break when Dad was ten. Grandma and Grandad never left, but Dad moved back to the UK for university.

I keep thinking back to the pink scarf at the audition. Had Grandma been there, watching me as a ghost? I wrap my arms around myself.

'The taxi is here!' calls Dad.

'Almost ready!' I say, flinging the last of my clothes into the suitcase. Dad had said to be prepared for all weather. Louisiana, where Grandma lived and the funeral is, will be hot, but he wants to take me on a road trip too. It's a trip that him and Grandma took almost every summer, from Louisiana all the way to Colorado, through four different states.

'I'm done!' I say, grabbing my suitcase and meeting him by the door.

We slide into the taxi. Dad rubs his palm across his forehead, looking tired. I know he didn't sleep last night, I heard him pacing up and down the hall.

Dad had told me more about what had happened during the shooting. A man had tried to rob a petrol station at gunpoint. The cashier couldn't get the till open and the gunman panicked and fired shots. Grandma was waiting in line to pay. I picture the scene and hope with all my might that she wasn't scared.

Grandma loved film and TV, especially the last scene before the credits. Nothing gave her more satisfaction than an uplifting ending to a movie and I can't shake the feeling that her own last few moments were far from what she would have wanted.

'I forgot to ask – how did your audition go?' Dad asks.

I hesitate. It feels like the audition happened in a separate life.

He's studying my face, searching for some breadcrumb of good news, of hope.

I can't bring myself to take that away from him.

Not now.

Not when his usually tall body is stooped and his smiling face is crumpled. Not when I know he's looking at me and seeing Grandma.

A lump settles in my throat and I bite the inside of my cheek to stop the tears. Why couldn't I have just remembered my stupid lines?

'It was great,' I say. My pulse quickens. 'Better than great. I got the part! They'll be in touch with you soon.' The words slip out before I can stop them. I just want to see him smile.

And he does. Dad beams. 'That's brilliant news! Grandma would be so proud.'

That makes me feel even worse.

'How long are we going to be in the States?' I ask, wanting to talk about something — anything — else.

'I was thinking two weeks. I want to take you on that road trip I used to do with Grandma every summer,' he replies. 'She was doing it alone when she died. We can finish it for her.'

He takes my hand and squeezes it, sending waves of guilt through my body. I always tell Dad the truth.

What would Grandma think if she could see me lying now?

I shake my head and pinch the skin above my nose, between my eyes. I miss Grandma. I miss her so much. She's the reason I wanted to act, the person I talked to the whole time Mum and Dad were getting divorced, and the only person who can make me feel like everything will be OK, even after a bad day. Without her, I don't know what I'll do. Who I am.

I'd do anything to get her back. Anything in the world.

Seb

Denver, Colorado

26th June, 9.15 a.m.

♥ THE THREE OF HEARTS ♥

Mom doesn't want to leave me at home alone so I'm running errands with her. A seagull squawks overhead and my mind drifts to the last game we played with Clay. Emily had tried to transform into an eagle to chase after Calamity, only she'd pulled a critical fail, and had transformed into a seagull instead, that then got distracted by food crumbs. We'd all laughed so much. I can't believe that was only last week.

We drive past the mall. That's where, two years ago, Mom told me that our dog, Buddy, had been run over outside our house. She wanted to wait until we got home but I could tell something was wrong from her tight lips and sad eyes and I kept asking her until she spilled.

I cried and cried and people stared. I hid my face but Mom told me not to worry about anyone looking. She stroked my hair and said to experience all emotion is to be human; it's what living is about. Which at the time I thought was a strange thing to say because I *was* human, whether I cried or not.

When I asked her what she meant, she said that it was important to acknowledge all the feelings, not just the happy ones.

To which I replied, 'Like elephants.'

And she looked a bit confused.

I explained that when elephants are sad, they

flap their ears against each other to show it. Clay had told me.

Inside the car, the turn signal ticks and Mom slows and changes lanes, leaving the mall behind us. I feel empty and my body is numb. I wish I could experience any emotion right now. Clutching my deck of cards, I instinctively shuffle them and pull one out, hoping for a high card.

The three of hearts.

That's pretty much a fail.

'Clay's dad told me that because it happened just outside of Denver, they're having a memorial for all the victims at the city hall there,' Mom says, interrupting my thoughts.

'That's good,' I say, but I wish she hadn't mentioned it. I turn to stare out of the window. I don't want to think about the incident today. I'll do anything not to think about it.

Mom pulls in to a gas station. Suddenly my chest feels like its full of water. My breathing quickens. It's as if I've gone from feeling no emotions to all of them at once.

I pull my knees to my chest.

Mom looks over at me and places her hand on my back. 'Are you OK?'

I shake my head.

'Oh honey, I'm so sorry, I didn't think.' She checks the gas gauge and sighs. 'We're almost out. I'll be really quick and I won't go inside. Just hang on.'

Without meaning to, I glance at the building and everything comes flooding back. I rock back and forth, my body filling with a hot anxiousness that sweeps from the pit of my stomach up through my chest until I'm clenching my jaw, my teeth pressing together. I try to stop the thoughts coming.

The gas station. The guy in the hoodie. The gunshots.

I pull my head down, holding it with my hands, trying to hide from the feelings engulfing me.

While the tank's filling Mom climbs in next to me and rubs my back. 'You're OK,' she tells me. 'You're OK.'

But I don't know if that's true. I don't think I'm OK at all.

Vivi

Lafayette, Louisiana
26th June, 11.35 a.m.

Grandma gave me my middle name. Aspen. It's her favourite tree.

When I was little, I'd curl up with her on the bench swing in her garden and she'd tell me the folktale of how people wore crowns made from aspen leaves to journey between our world and the spirit world and back again safely.

The aeroplane doors open and the first thing that hits me is the heat and the humidity. I feel sticky.

Dad's rented a car and he puts on his baseball cap as he gets into the driver's seat. We leave the airport and travel along wide roads, past huge billboard signs and underneath long power lines.

'Almost there,' he says after half an hour. 'Do you remember the way to Grandma's house?'

I nod. It's only been two years since we came for Thanksgiving.

We enter a neighbourhood filled with leafy trees. The American flag flies outside some of the houses. The front gardens are all neat and tidy and mailboxes line the side of the road.

The knot in my stomach is back by the time we reach Grandma's house. She moved here with Grandad to get away from the busy city of Los Angeles when Dad was a teenager, and stayed here even after Grandad died. A huge oak tree stands in the front garden with the wooden bench swing hanging from it. I get out of the car and stretch, stiff from all the travelling.

My Aunt Maggie comes running out of the house to greet us. 'Vivi!' she says, grabbing me and squeezing me tightly. 'I've put you in the Blue Room, as usual,' Aunt Maggie says. The Blue Room was always my room when I would come and stay with Grandma.

'Josh!' She turns to Dad and they hug. I look around, half-expecting Grandma to be on the swing, even though I know she can't be. To the side of the house, bright cream flowers dot a big leafy tree. The magnolias are in bloom. They're Grandma's favourite flowers. I walk up to the tree and sniff one of the gigantic flowers on the tip of a twig. It smells lemony and fresh.

'It feels so strange without Mimi here,' I hear Aunt Maggie say behind me.

'I know. Do you need my help with anything before tomorrow?' asks Dad.

I leave Dad talking about the funeral with Aunt Maggie and climb the steps to the porch before going inside. It's instantly chilly with the air conditioning and big fans whirring overhead. I untie my cardigan from my waist and slip it on. The curtains are moving back and forth in the wind from the fans, just like the Spanish moss on the big oak tree outside the window which is swaying in the breeze.

There's a thump from one of the back rooms. I didn't think anyone else was here yet, apart from Aunt Maggie.

'Grandma?' I whisper. 'Is that you?'

There's no response but I have a feeling that I'm not alone in the house.

I brush it off and quickly take my bag to the Blue Room. It smells of fresh linen. Each of the bedrooms are painted different colours. Across the hall, the door to Grandma's room is open and I take a deep breath and step inside. The walls are pink, just like her scarf.

Something moves on her bed and I jump and shriek. Curled up on her pillow is a ferret.

'Bandit!' I say, rushing over to stroke him. His long, slender body is covered in shades of brown fur. He has a cone-shaped nose and a cream face with a mask of dark brown hair over his eyes. He's curled up around a collection of Grandma's things: an earring; a penny; a paperclip; and a broken bracelet.

I didn't know Bandit would still be here. I'd imagined someone would have taken him to look after. Grandma's had him since he was a baby, a kit — almost six years. I attempt the clicking sound Grandma used to make to call him and he lifts his head, squeaks and then dives head first into my sleeve. I bring him close to my body and give him a cuddle. His head pokes out the top of my cardigan.

'I bet you're missing her,' I say softly. 'I am too.'

Seb

Denver, Colorado
28th June, 1 p.m.

♥ THE SIX OF HEARTS ♥

Christine, the therapist, is smiley and dressed in jeans and a t-shirt, with purple thread woven into her braids. I slouch into the chair. This is my first session. It was Mom's idea, to help with my problem. Anxiety attacks, she calls them. I don't know what they are, just that they keep happening. Out of nowhere, they bubble up and overwhelm me.

Thinking about going to Yellowstone and helping Clay sometimes stops them before they get too bad because it makes me feel like I'll see him really soon, and I know I'd never have an anxiety attack around Clay.

But I won't make it there if I can't go through a gas station, or pass a bus on the highway without panicking.

'What are the things which trigger an attack?' Christine asks, leaning forward.

'Gas stations,' I reply. 'Buses. Loud noises. And the idea of going to the memorial.'

'And how do you feel when you think about them now?'

I shuffle in my seat and look down. I don't want to talk about it, but if I'm going to help Clay I know I need to try. I force the words out. Heat flares along the tips of my ears and the back of my neck.

'Scared. I never want to go to a gas station again,' I say, linking and unlinking my hands. 'I want to go to the memorial, but I don't think I can.'

The memorial is a big one. I want to show my support to everyone there but when I think about it my throat tightens and my palms get sweaty.

She nods. 'I want to help you understand what's happening in your body when you're having an attack,' she says gently. 'When you were on the bus, your body rightly identified that you were in danger and activated your flight or fight response.'

I nod. *Obviously*, I think.

'It's an evolutionary adaptation to help you survive. But now your brain is triggering the fight or flight response every time you go to a gas station or when something reminds you of the incident.'

'So how do I turn that off?' I ask, hoping it's something easy.

'It's not as simple as turning it off like a light switch,' Christine says, smiling. 'But there are some things that can help.'

I nod again. I'll try anything.

'The first is mindful breathing. That just means being aware of your own breath. You might find it helpful to count your exhales. We can give you some exercises to work on.' Her voice is calm and relaxing.

'Another tool is mentally distancing yourself from your emotions. Rather than letting the feeling of being unsafe take over, you can say to yourself, "I'm having the *thought* that it's unsafe." But don't try to fight yourself. Observe your feelings. What are they telling you? Be willing to have those tough feelings and let them come and go.' She leans forward and gestures in a circle, imitating the feelings coming and going.

It's a lot to take in at once so I just nod. I'll try; I have to. I can't be scared of gas stations for ever.

I have to get to that rainbow pool.

I want Clay to get better.

'What if those two things don't help?' I ask.

'The third tool you can try is to list five things you can see, four things you can feel, three things you can hear, two things you can smell and one thing you can taste. You can do this anywhere but it can be very especially effective if you're outside. Focusing on the nature around you can help take your mind off of your anxiety. Some people even find it helpful to list things they know, like the states of America or different vegetables or something like that.'

I straighten my back at the mention of nature. Yellowstone is *very* much in nature.

Now I have three tools to help. One of them is bound to work, right? Sliding my hand into my pocket, my palm closes around my deck of cards.

'You said something about nature,' I say. 'Is spending time in nature a good idea?'

'I think that would be a brilliant idea. I know I always find nature very healing,' Christine replies, clasping her hands together.

A plan forms in my mind.

I sneak a peek at the top card of my deck. It's the six of hearts. A fifty-fifty chance of my plan succeeding.

'Let's talk to my mom about that,' I say. 'Can I get her?'

'Sure,' says Christine, though she sounds surprised.

Outside I grab Mom's arm excitedly. 'There's something I want to talk to you about.'

'OK,' she says, startled. She lets me lead her into the room and sits down.

'Can we go to Yellowstone?' I ask. 'We've agreed that some time in nature is EXACTLY what I need and it's what Clay would want me to do. I know it. And you haven't had a vacation in ages.'

Mom looks baffled. She glances between me and Christine, who is frowning. 'What about the gas stations on the way?'

'I know three techniques that can stop the anxiety attacks now,' I say, trying to reassure her.

'Do *you* think this is a good idea?' Mom asks Christine.

'Spending time outside is a good idea,' Christine says slowly, looking at me curiously, 'but it doesn't have to be all the way in Yellowstone.'

'Please,' I say to Mom. 'I want to get out of the city.' It's what Mom says to her friends when they go camping together.

I can't mention the rainbow pool, not yet.

Mom strokes my head, looking concerned, but nods. 'Let me talk to work,' she says. 'I'm owed a few days off.'

'YES,' I say and squeeze my fists in celebration. Now I just have to convince Mom to make the wish with me, but I'll worry about that when we get there. Surely once we're in Yellowstone Park she won't say no.

Vivi

St. Martinville, Louisiana

29th June, 8.30 a.m.

It's the day of Grandma's funeral. Bandit won't come out from my cardigan. He keeps peeking his head up, as if he's looking for her, then retreating inside.

'What's going to happen to him?' I ask Dad, as we get ready at the house.

He's concentrating on his tie. 'Maybe there's a shelter we can take him to?'

I frown. Ferrets can die of loneliness. I remember Grandma telling me that. She said they're highly sociable creatures. I can't let her ferret die!

'He's coming with me,' I say, and I stroke his soft nose. Bandit looks up at me with big eyes.

Dad's never let me have a pet before, unless you count the hamster that escaped after five days. He usually says we're too busy. But to my surprise, he leans forward and tickles Bandit under the chin and says, 'I think it will be good for all of us to have this little fella with us.'

Dad turns to straighten his tie in the mirror and I raise Bandit to my face and whisper, 'Do you hear that? We get to stay together from now on.'

He snuggles against my neck.

'Can I wear something of Grandma's today?' I ask, wanting to feel even closer to her.

'Why don't you choose a pair of earrings?' suggests Dad.

I pick a silver dangly pair with opals at the end.

'They're perfect,' says Dad.

I think back to the audition and the woman's pink scarf. I wonder if Grandma was really there, watching me. Had she been disappointed in me? I bet she never forgot her lines.

I stare at the pictures of her dotted around the living room. With her white hair that looked like whipped cream and wise eyes that sparkled, she had an aura about her that said to never question her authority. If only I'd inherited that part of her too.

My eyes land on a photo from Thanksgiving two years ago. I remember that day. The huge amount of food she laid out for us, the slight tremble of her hand as she served it and her laughter as we all chatted and ate together. I hug Bandit close. It will never be the same again.

At the funeral, I weave in and out of the sea of black clothes to the front of the church. My cousin Rose puts her arm around my shoulders when Dad reads the eulogy. His voice wavers as he speaks.

'She was an unstoppable force. I've never known anyone with her positivity and acceptance of the ups and downs of life . . .'

I wish I could be more like Grandma.

After the funeral, the family gathers at the house and in the yard. Everyone keeps coming up to me and asking about how my acting's going.

'Come meet Vivi,' says Rose to her boyfriend. 'She's the one that inherited Grandma's talent.'

There's that word again. *Talent.*

'She just got a starring role!' Dad calls over.

I force a smile and tell them about the audition and how I got the part. The lies keep on coming, as if they have a life of their own. I can't stop them. I tell every person I see.

I retreat inside the house and overhear Dad talking to his friend. 'I just don't even understand how this could have happened. How do you move forward after this?'

I leave them and wander over to Grandma's piano. I gingerly touch the keys she played so many times. Debussy was her favourite pianist. She taught me one of his pieces. I sit, placing my foot on the pedal. I bring my fingers down over the keys and play the first notes. They cascade over me like a trickle of water.

And then the tears come. I keep playing as they drip down my cheek and onto the keys. I miss her so much it hurts in my stomach. Every part of me longs to hug her. I have so much love for her and nowhere to put it.

The piece finishes and I sit there for a minute. When I turn to get up, I notice Dad watching from the doorway. He wipes both eyes with the palms of his hands.

♠ ♣ ♥ ♦

Later, Dad sits down on the swing seat and beckons me to sit next to him.

'A whole generation of children have sat under this tree,' he says, smiling and patting the swing. 'I want to show you something. Wait here.'

He gets up and walks to the garage, opening the door. Inside is a car hidden underneath a sheet, covered in dust.

I cough as he pulls it off and dust fills the air, sparkling in the shafts of sunlight.

'Ta da!' he says, unveiling a black Cadillac. 'This is the car that me and your grandma used to drive on our road trips to Colorado. And now we're going to drive it on ours! Meet Cormac the Cadillac!'

'It's a bit old, isn't it?' I say, concerned.

'Yes, but Cormac's got style *and* charisma. He fits Mimi perfectly, don't you think?'

I laugh. The car *is* very Grandma. 'How long is the road trip going to take?' I ask.

'Well, I just found out there's going to be a memorial for the victims in Denver, in two days' time, so I think we should leave tomorrow and go to that. It means we'll have to drive there quickly but we can take our time and stop at all the sights on the way back.'

'Oh,' I say, feeling mixed about the memorial. It will be nice to have another chance to remember Grandma but it sounds very sad too.

Dad starts packing camping gear into the boot of the car. 'Those road trips were some of the best times in my life,' he says.

I roll my eyes. 'Spending twenty hours in a car sounds exactly how I'd want to spend a holiday,' I say sarcastically. Dad and I always tease each other and I hope my comment will make him smile.

'Hey!' says Dad, laughing. 'Just you wait. You'll love it.'

A tiny spark of joy explodes in my chest that I can still make him laugh. Maybe this trip will be good for both of us.

Seb

Denver, Colorado

29th June, 5.30 p.m.

♥ THE NINE OF HEARTS ♥

When we did our school project on Yellowstone, Clay was fascinated by the wolves.

He learnt how they'd been reintroduced back into the park in 1995, even though lots of people didn't want wolves around. And when they were reintroduced, an amazing thing happened: the wolves hunted the elk, which meant the elk avoided areas where they couldn't keep watch for the wolves, which meant more plants and trees could grow, which in turn led to a recovery of the beaver population, which had almost disappeared completely.

I smile, remembering Clay explaining it to the rest of the class. Yellowstone is full of weird and wonderful things. There are even microorganisms which live in thermal pools that are over 200 degrees Celsius! If there's anywhere my wish has a chance of coming true, it's there.

'Are you sure you want to do this?' asks Mom. We're in the car port, digging out our camping gear.

'Of course!' I say. Going to Yellowstone is the only thing that makes sense right now.

I pull out my deck of cards from my pocket. My deck is made up of cards from four different packs, all with different backs. Mine had pictures of dragons on them, Emily's were classic, Ava's had watermelons on them, and Zac's had dogs.

The thing I like about our game is that if

you're paying attention to the cards and you haven't picked any good cards in a while, then you know there's a high probability of drawing a good card next, so you can try something really risky.

I think about Clay, waiting for his operation. Mom told me that the specialist arrived and said they now have to wait for Clay to become more stable before they operate. I wonder what the probability of him surviving is. If I can make it to the rainbow pool, his chances have got to go up. I can influence it, just like in the game.

I take a deep breath and turn over the top card. It's a nine of hearts. 'Yes!' I say. A HIGH chance of success!

'Everything OK?' asks Mom.

'IT'S GOING TO BE!' I shout back.

Vivi

Amarillo, Texas

30th June, 6 a.m.

I bring a pair of Grandma's sunglasses and one of her scarves with me, and on the first day of the trip, when the sun's high enough in the sky, I put them on and wind the window down so I can stick out my elbow and lean on it. The wind rushes against my face. Everything is yellow tinted. I can see why Grandma enjoyed this!

A huge lorry rumbles behind us. I glance in the rearview mirror. Its headlights look like eyes. As it passes I hold my breath. Its number plate says Washington State, thousands of miles away.

'Eighteen-wheelers,' mutters Dad, as it overtakes us. 'Terrifying things.'

The drive through Texas takes for ever. It just goes on and on and on. I keep seeing the same five things out of the window: flat fields; oil pumps; wind farms; cow farms; and huge, robot-like crop-watering machines. And repeat. Nothing changes apart from the ground, which gets redder and drier the further we go. I fall asleep and when I wake up it's exactly the same.

'I thought there were supposed to be cool landmarks and things like that,' I say. 'This is all a bit rubbish.'

'Just you wait until the way back when we'll have time to explore,' says Dad. He glances over at me. I lean my head against the window and close my eyes.

'Don't go to sleep again,' he says. 'You just woke up.'

'What else am I supposed to do?' I ask. Bandit is curled up on my lap.

'Grandma and I used to play games. I Spy?'

'Dad, I'm not five,' I reply.

'Twenty Questions?'

I sigh.

'Humour me,' says Dad. He slows as we pass a road sign. 'Oh, wait a minute,' he says. 'You're saved. This is the town where Grandma and I used to eat every trip, always at the same restaurant. It was delicious. It's called Lulu's House.'

'Good timing,' I say. 'I'm starving.'

'Just wait until you see this place,' says Dad.

He takes the next turn off the main road and drives through a sparse town, leaning forwards and peering through the windscreen at the shops and restaurants lining the high street. When we reach the end, he turns around and drives back again.

'Are we lost?' I ask.

'I know it's around here somewhere. Maybe it was off the main road. It's been so long now . . .' He sounds confused.

He drives up the side streets too.

'You've got to be kidding me,' says Dad, under his breath.

'What now?' I ask.

'I can't find it,' says Dad, pulling into a parking spot.

'Let's just go somewhere else,' I say, hungry.

But when I look over at Dad he's crying.

'We can keep searching for the restaurant,' I say gently, feeling bad. 'But it had better have the best food I've ever tasted.'

Dad smiles. 'I just can't believe it's gone.' He wipes his eyes. 'I wanted this trip to be exactly like it was when me and your grandma did it. But of course, it's not going to be the same! She would be laughing at me right now and saying, "What's all this nonsense?" Everything changes.'

I laugh with him and reach over and hold his hand. Bandit stirs on my lap.

'Why don't we go to that place?' I ask, pointing at a café with people sitting outside.

'Perfect. But keep Bandit hidden,' he adds, giving the ferret a 'you–better–behave' type of look.

I place Bandit in my shoulder bag. He turns in circles to get comfy, then curls up again. Grandma said ferrets have unique personalities. One thing about Bandit is that he loves to sleep.

'Can I do the ordering?' I ask, as we're walking up to the counter. It smells of tomato soup and toast.

'Sure!' says Dad.

'Bonjour,' I say in my best French accent to the woman by the till.

She looks up and smiles. 'Can I take your order?'

I inspect the cakes and pastries. 'We would like zee blueberry muffin and zee strawberry pie. Zey look delicious.'

I glance at Dad to see if I'm making him smile. When I was younger I loved to pretend I was a tourist with him and talk in loads of different accents. I haven't done it in years.

It's working. Dad's smiling as he joins in. 'Zank you very much,' he says, in his attempt at a French accent. 'And two Mediterranean sandwiches as well.'

'Coming right up,' says the lady.

I grin. I can't believe she bought our accents. And Dad is smiling again.

After our lunch stop, Dad drives as far as he can until he gets tired. He keeps one hand on the steering wheel, the other on his knee, gently tapping his fingers and nodding his head to the songs on the radio.

That night we stay in a motel. I lie on the bed and flick through the TV channels with Bandit sprawled out next to me.

I think about earlier and how much I enjoyed pretending to be French with Dad. I stroke the soft fur on Bandit's head. There are so many things I wanted to do with Grandma, so many things I want to ask her now that she's gone. Why did she get a ferret? Did she ever fail at any auditions? Did she ever forget her lines?

'I've been saving this to give to you,' says Dad, lifting a wrapped present from his suitcase. 'It's from Grandma. She'd already got you a present for your birthday. I found it at the house.'

My birthday isn't for a month. I take the present and examine her curly handwriting on the tag.

To Vivi, with love, Grandma.

I take the tag and put it in my pocket. I turn the present over and carefully open it along the line of tape. It's a shoe box and inside is a chunky pair of trainers.

A few months ago, Grandma and I had been on the phone to each other as we watched the British Film Awards. Kestrel Otterman, the actor, came on stage wearing the most amazing pair of trainers. We both agreed I'd look fabulous in them, but I never expected to actually own a pair!

I smile and hug them. They have that new shoe smell, rubber and canvas. Bandit thinks the shoe box is a present for him and scampers in and out of it.

Seb

Denver, Colorado

1st July, 7.15 a.m.

♥ THE TWO OF HEARTS ♥

Today's the day of the memorial for the victims of the shooting.

We're going to leave for Yellowstone straight afterwards.

Mom and I load the car. I've packed my camping clothes, mosquito spray, bear spray, two flashlights, my rain gear and my camera — so I can show Clay that I went.

I slide Clay's handbook from my backpack and open it to the last page.

FINDING THE RAINBOW POOL.

Some hints for the adventurers:
1. It's in the south-west of the park.
2. It's deep blue in the middle and red on the outside, with rings of rainbow colours between.
3. It's huge, bigger than a football field.

Based on geography and images I've found of the pools, I think the rainbow pool he's describing could be one of two places: the Morning Glory Pool or the Grand Prismatic Spring.

I still haven't told Mom the real reason that I want to go to Yellowstone. I think it will just worry her.

'I know we're doing this trip because of the awful things that have happened,' says Mom as she puts our tents into the trunk. 'But I'm so excited to take this trip with you, just the two of us.'

I nod. 'Me too.'

'And Dad will be with us in spirit,' she says, and touches her necklace. 'How are you feeling about the memorial?'

'OK,' I say, although the truth is I'm doing everything I can to avoid thinking about it. Every time I do, my chest fills with unease. I've tried to do the breathing exercise the therapist taught me. She said it was important to practise, but it's easier to just avoid thinking about it until I have to.

'Are you sure you're going to be OK with the drive and the gas stations?' asks Mom. 'If you're finding it too much we can come straight home.'

'I'll be fine. I don't think I'll get any more attacks,' I say, although I don't really believe that. I pause. 'Mom? If I ask you to do something at Yellowstone, do you promise to ask no questions and just do it?'

She looks up at me, her eyebrows concerned, and readjusts her orange headband. 'Seb, you're definitely going to have to tell me what this is about.'

I decide to just come out and tell her. 'There's

a rainbow pool there that Clay really wanted to see. I want to go and find it.'

'That's a lovely thing to do!' says Mom, clapping her hands together. 'Why didn't you want to tell me that?'

'Because when we're there we . . . both have to wish that he gets better.' I try and say it quickly under my breath, but she hears.

'Oh, darling,' Mom says sadly. 'You know that wishing isn't going to make a difference.'

Ever since Dad died, she's been very practical.

'Wishes aren't real,' she says, gently taking hold of my shoulders. 'You'd blame yourself if it doesn't work.'

'I won't,' I reply. 'I'll just know that I tried everything to make him better. Besides, he's going to be fine. I know it. Especially if I go there and we make the wish.'

She meets my eyes and says, 'Oh, Seb.'

Mom and I are so connected that I know instantly when she's not saying something. (A bit like my telepathic character in the game — but in real life my superpower only works with her.)

'What is it?' I ask. 'What aren't you saying?'

'Honey, Clay was hurt very badly,' she says. 'The doctors are doing all they can. But there's a possibility he won't be OK.'

'NO,' I say. My voice comes out louder than I mean it to. I put the last of my things in the trunk and slam it shut. I take a deep breath. 'Can we just go, please?'

'Sweetie, I'm not sure going to the memorial right now is such a good idea. You're clearly upset. I'm worried about you.'

When I think about going to the memorial, my stomach churns. When I think about *not* going to the memorial, my stomach churns. Both options are awful. But I was there when the shooting happened and going is the right thing to do. I want to show my respects, to say goodbye, even though it's difficult.

'This is something I need to do,' I say.

She nods and smiles. 'Then I'll be right by your side.'

'Thanks,' I say, but now all I can think about is that I'll have to come up with a different plan for the wish. I can tell Mom isn't going to do it, and I need to find someone to make the wish with me. Unless I can change Mom's mind . . .

I pull the top card from my deck. The two of hearts. A low chance of me being able to persuade her. Anyway, I don't think Mom's wish would even count if she didn't believe in it.

Vivi

Pueblo, Colorado

1st July, 8 a.m.

Dad pulls over at a café an hour after we cross the state border into Colorado. We sit outside and drink iced tea and coffee. Bandit nudges my hand with his nose to tell me he wants to run around so I put his lead on and walk with him on the grass next to us.

Dad yawns and rubs his eyes.

'Tired?' I ask.

He nods. 'I think it's the emotions of everything catching up with me more than anything else.'

'Makes sense,' I say. I'd heard him snoring last night while I lay awake. I'd had an opera song stuck in my head and wondered whether it was because of Grandma's presence.

'Do you believe in ghosts?' I ask.

'Why?' asks Dad. 'Did you see Grandma?'

'More like I kind of . . . *felt* her.'

He nods. 'I've felt her with us too. Just because her body has gone doesn't mean there aren't parts of her still here. Like her love of performing, which she passed down to you.'

There it is again. I have to be successful. More than ever now that she's gone.

We set off, back on the road. After a few hours, the scenery begins to change. The flat highways turn into steep slopes and inclines through wooded cliffsides. We turn a corner and I glimpse mountains in the distance. Coming into

Denver, we hit traffic. It's ten o'clock. The service starts in under an hour.

'We're not going to have time to stop at the hotel and change before the memorial,' Dad says. 'We'll have to change at a petrol station.' He pulls in.

In the cramped station toilets I slip on a long navy dress and brush my short bob with my fingers. If I use a hairbrush my slight curls become frizzy waves. Dad watches Bandit for me outside while I change.

He looks funny in his suit holding a ferret. Bandit has decided he likes to wrap himself around Dad's neck like a scarf.

I slip Bandit off his neck and put him in his cage for a while. Cormac the Cadillac is absolutely packed to the rim but I've managed to find a place for it balanced between our bags on the back seat.

The traffic clears and our car speeds along the road towards the city centre.

'We're making good time,' says Dad, checking his watch.

And then the car splutters, lurches and completely loses steam. It gets slower and slower. We're on a busy road and cars honk and zoom past us.

'What's happening?' I ask.

'I think we're breaking down,' says Dad. He presses the emergency lights and pulls over.

'You think?' I ask, as the car comes to a complete halt.

'Yes, we are definitely breaking down,' says Dad.

'I knew it was a bad idea to drive this old car,' I say.

'This car is a classic. It's dependable. I'm sure I'll be able to fix it,' says Dad, climbing out and opening the bonnet.

'I'll wait on the grass,' I say, taking Bandit and sliding out. I grab the cut magnolias I took for the memorial too.

'It's all part of the adventure, as Grandma would say,' Dad tells me, his voice muffled. 'We always had car trouble on our trips.'

I sit on the grassy verge, thankful there is one. The grass twitches around me. Are there rattlesnakes here?

'What do you think?' I ask Bandit. 'Is there a rattlesnake nearby?' Bandit stands on his back legs and turns his head from side to side.

Next to the car, Dad runs his hands though his hair.

'Any idea what the matter is?' I ask.

'Everything looks fine,' he says, exasperated. 'I don't know.'

'It was a while ago we stopped for petrol,' I say, thinking back.

'But the gauge said the tank was full — hang on!' Dad says. 'The gauge must have broken.'

'What do we do now?' I ask.

'This,' he says and he sticks his hand out at the passing cars, trying to wave one down.

Seb

Denver, Colorado

1st July, 10.30 a.m.

 THE SEVEN OF HEARTS

We're running late for the memorial. It starts in thirty minutes and Mom can't find her car keys. I pull a seven of hearts. It's likely we'll make it, but there will be some obstacles in the way.

'I think I put them down while we were sorting through the camping stuff,' she says, lifting up pieces of paper and clothes and checking underneath.

I'm starting to feel that tightness in my chest again. A tiny part of me is hoping that she doesn't find her keys in time and we miss the memorial.

'I know they have to be here somewhere,' Mom says, a bit more frantically now. 'What was I wearing before I got changed?' She rummages in the pockets of her jeans, which are on the bed amongst a pile of discarded clothes. 'Found them!'

I bite my bottom lip. We have to go now. We leave the house and I take a deep breath before climbing into the car.

Just before we make it to the city centre, I notice an old Cadillac pulled over on the side of the road. A man waves his arm at us as we approach.

Mom slows.

'We're already late,' I say. 'Do we have to stop?'

A part of me is worried that if we stop now,

I won't find the strength to go to the memorial.

'It will just take a second,' Mom says. 'If we can help them, then we will. If not, at least we'll have tried, right? Besides, it's more important now than ever to be kind to people. Look how worried that poor girl looks.'

'Please, Mom,' I say.

Mum ignores me, pulls over behind them and winds down the window. 'You all right there?'

The man runs up. He has floppy blonde hair. The girl stands up. 'Thanks so much for stopping. We ran out of petrol and we're supposed to be at a memorial.'

'You're going to a memorial?' asks Mom, surprised. 'For the shooting?'

He nods. 'Yes.'

'We're headed there too,' says Mom. She checks her watch. 'It's getting late. Why don't you ride with us there and then we'll help you get your car running afterwards?'

'You're a lifesaver,' says the man. He wipes the grease off his hands and holds one out to Mom. 'I'm Josh and this is my daughter, Vivi.

'Nice to meet you,' says Mom. 'This is Seb and I'm Charlie.'

'Hi,' Vivi says as she climbs into the back. She has a British accent and big green eyes that glance over our camping gear. Mom starts the car and we pull out.

Something moves in her bag. A flash of brown. 'Ahhh!' I shout. 'There's a rat or something in your bag!'

She smiles and pulls out a long-bodied creature. 'Not a rat,' she says. 'A ferret. He's called Bandit. He belonged to my grandma. She was in the shooting.'

I stiffen at the word. I've been calling it 'the incident'. Images of the gas station, a gun, Clay, race through my head.

'Are you OK?' Vivi asks.

I nod and stare at the animal. It takes me a few seconds to be convinced that she really isn't holding a rat. I've never seen a ferret in real life before.

Mom is chatting away to Josh. Their conversation wafts from the front of the car. I realise I still haven't responded to Vivi.

'I'm sorry for your loss,' I say, awkwardly.

'Thanks,' Vivi says. 'Did you know someone who got shot too?'

'My best friend was there,' I say. 'He's in the hospital.'

'I hope he makes a speedy recovery,' Vivi says. 'You want to stroke Bandit?' She holds up the ferret.

I reach out and stroke his soft fur. It calms my racing heart.

It's a summer day in Denver and as we drive

through the city, everyone is out, gathered in groups on the sidewalk, laughing and chatting. We pass the forty-foot Blue Bear sculpture, of the big blue bear looking through the Colorado Convention Centre. A bunch of tourists are photographing it from different angles.

'Vivi, look!' says Josh, turning from the front. 'Grandma loved that sculpture.'

Vivi smiles and gazes at it as we pass.

A few minutes later Mom pulls into a car park of a town hall. 'Here we are,' she says.

Outside the building a group of people have gathered. They hold signs that say ENOUGH IS ENOUGH and NO MORE GUNS.

I quickly avert my gaze. I can't think about guns right now.

A man is playing the cello as we enter. The room is quiet and the low string notes fill the space. Alongside one wall is a collection of flowers, notes, and photographs of everyone who died. Candles flicker, illuminating the pictures. It smells of matches and mint lemonade. Rows of seats fill the rest of the room.

Mom turns and studies my face. 'Are you OK?' she says quietly.

'I'm totally fine,' I say but I can't bring myself to look at the photographs. Not yet. Seven people died. I wasn't one of them, but I could have been.

Vivi kneels by the photographs and arranges her flowers.

'Seb,' says a voice I recognise. It's Mr Evans. He looks tired. 'How are you?'

Seeing him brings everything back in a rush and suddenly I'm crouching in the bus, staring into his eyes again as he holds me down and tells me it's going to be OK.

I manage to shrug. 'Gonna get some water,' I mumble.

'It's good to see you,' he says, as I stumble away. I search for Mom, not wanting her to wander too far from me. She's walking ahead, talking to Josh. I feel overwhelmed, drowning in fear. I try to count my breaths, like Christine said to do. In for one, two, three, four, out for one, two, three, four.

It's not working. I can still feel the panic rising up.

What's the second exercise?

It's something about focusing on my emotions but I'm swallowed in them. I head for the snack table, desperate for something to distract me. I grab a cup. Maybe a glass of lemonade will help.

People are sitting down now, someone steps onto the stage and calls for quiet.

'There you are,' says Mom, finding me and ushering me to a chair. I sit down shakily.

Mom said earlier there would be readings

from the victims' families and people who were there and survived. Clay could have been one of the people in these photos. Or I could have been. I replay the probabilities and possibilities:

If I hadn't cut in line.

If I'd waited for Clay inside.

If we had driven to a different gas station.

The word *Clay* penetrates my thoughts. There's a different man onstage now. 'He tried to protect her,' he's saying. 'He tried to protect that woman.'

Was he talking about Clay? A ringing starts in my ears. Everything gets blurry at the edges. I stare and focus on the bubbles rising and popping in my lemonade.

Lemonade. That's what the old lady was drinking. She wanted a nice cold can from the back of the fridge . . .

I get out my pack and organise the cards. I gather all the aces, the twos, the threes . . . Everything in the background becomes a blur.

There's a hand on my shoulder and I jump. It's Mom. My vision focuses. There are no more speakers and people are leaving the hall. Vivi and her dad are standing next to us.

'We were thinking about all getting lunch together,' Mom says. 'What do you feel like?'

'Anything,' I say. I just want to get out of the town hall.

Vivi

Denver, Colorado
1st July, 1.30 p.m.

We sit inside a Mexican restaurant, underneath a string of fairy lights. My mind goes over the memorial. One of the speakers had been there that day. He told us how brave everyone had been inside the gas station. He even said that Grandma told the shooter to drop the gun. I can picture her saying it, loud and clear: *Drop the gun*. If only the shooter had listened to her.

And apparently Seb's friend had tried to push Grandma out of the way before she was hurt.

Knowing more about Grandma's last moments being filled with courage and kindness settles the unease I've had in my stomach since I heard about the shooting.

Grandma would have enjoyed the memorial, down to the activists outside.

The same speaker had said that you don't know how you're going to act until you're in that situation yourself.

I wonder how I would act?

The server places glasses of water and baskets of tortilla chips with salsa on the table.

Seb seems quiet. He keeps gazing into the distance with his deep, dark eyes. I wonder if he's shy or just doesn't feel like talking. Our parents are chatting enough for the both of us though. Dad's telling Charlie about our road trip.

'An event like the shooting causes a "before" and an "after",' he says. 'Vivi's Grandma always said that life was wonderful and I wanted the immediate "after" of her life to be wonderful too. So . . . we're going to do a big tour of places she loved. We're camping in Aspen, then visiting Glenwood Springs before turning around and stopping at a few places on the way back to Louisiana. Anywhere else you can recommend around here?'

'Well, we're going camping too – in Yellowstone Park,' says Charlie. Her expression is relaxed. Dark freckles dot her nose and cheekbones. 'Apparently it's amazing,' she continues. 'We've never actually been before, even though it's not too far from here.'

'It's a supervolcano,' says Seb, suddenly chiming in.

'That could be exciting!' says Dad, and he looks at me.

I glare back at him.

'Why don't you come with us?' asks Charlie.

I frown at Dad, who is smiling widely. He's not seriously going to say 'yes' is he? This is *our* road trip, something special that he wanted to share with *me*. Seb and his mum seem fine, but this is our way of saying goodbye to Grandma.

I try to communicate this with my eyes, but Dad is grinning at Charlie. 'That sounds lovely, if you don't mind us tagging along. Vivi was just saying the trip needed livening up a bit.'

'Do we have time?' I ask. 'Didn't you want to stop at the sights on the way back?'

'I think visiting a supervolcano trumps the steak-eating contest I was going to show you. You wanted to create our own memories. This is perfect!'

It's most definitely *not* perfect.

Charlie and Dad smile at each other as our plans for a special road trip slip away. *Great.*

'Did you ever participate in the steak-eating contest?' asks Charlie.

'Oh yes,' says Dad. They're laughing.

I want to roll my eyes at them.

'What was it like?' she asks.

'It's this weird place, right? It has animal heads all over the walls.' Dad's always been a storyteller. He's good at it too. 'My mom dared me to try and the whole restaurant watched me eat on this raised platform. And I could only manage a quarter of it!'

Charlie smiles.

Seb's pulling a face at her.

'I don't eat meat any more though,' says Dad.

'Wait,' I say, thinking of a way to get Dad back on our plan. 'I still want to go to the campground you were telling me about. The one you and Grandma visited.'

'Oh yeah,' says Dad. 'We have to do that. Would you guys fancy it too?' He turns back to

Charlie. 'It will only add a few hours on to the drive.'

'Sounds like a plan!' says Charlie.

I groan internally.

The server brings our drinks and I hide Bandit under the table.

Dad lifts his glass into the middle of the table, his face glowing and smiling. 'To kindness and new friendships in times of darkness,' he says.

'To fun times,' I add sarcastically.

Dad says, 'Cheers,' and doesn't even notice my tone. I'm done feeling positive and all I can think is that this stupid city is one of the last places Grandma ever saw.

Seb

Denver, Colorado
1st July, 1.45 p.m.

♥ THE JACK OF HEARTS ♥

I don't know WHAT just happened but somehow Mom went from helping Vivi and her dad out with their car to inviting them to Yellowstone with us.

Vivi doesn't look pleased; she has a single eyebrow raised and is staring almost in disbelief at her dad. I'm pretty sure she was trying to tell him that she doesn't want to come to Yellowstone. She keeps tucking one of her short springy curls of hair behind her ears only to have it pop back out.

One thing's for certain; dinner has taken my mind off the memorial and the incident. The waves of anxiety have passed and I'm beginning to feel like myself again. I might even be able to eat the fajita in front of me.

I slip my hand into my pocket and feel the comforting shape of my deck of cards. Vivi's ferret jumps at me and dives head first into my pocket. 'OH NO!' I say, yanking my hand out of the way.

'He thinks you've got treats,' Vivi says.

'Just a deck of cards,' I say, gently pulling the ferret out and showing him the deck.

'Oh, I love cards!' Vivi says. 'I used to play rummy with Grandma.'

'Do you have a favourite card?' I ask.

Vivi thinks for a second. 'The jack of hearts.'

'No waaaay,' I say, my heart rocketing. 'Mine's

the ten of hearts.' What are the chances her favourite card is so close to mine?

She smiles at me.

An idea comes to me then. I wasn't sure about Vivi coming to Yellowstone with us at first, but she likes cards and maybe I can ask her if she'll make the wish at the rainbow pool with me. That would solve everything.

Vivi

Aspen, Colorado

2nd July, 3 p.m.

The next day, Charlie drives us to go to buy petrol and we get Cormac the Cadillac running again. Then Dad and I pack up our stuff and set out for Independence Pass, the mountain road to Aspen, with Seb and Charlie following us in their car.

This mountain pass is only open in summer. I glance behind me through the back mirror. Seb and his mum are still driving right behind us.

Last night, once Seb started talking, he didn't stop. It turns out he's not quiet at all; his voice is *loud*. He told me all about the geology of Yellowstone and a game that he created with his friends. It sounded fun, kind of a cross between storytelling and acting. He said it was called Calamity Stoppers and that his friend Clay was the Game Master, Wolfie.

Once I got to know Seb more, the idea of travelling with them didn't seem so bad. I'd never admit this to Dad but it might even be fun to have them on our trip. Besides, Dad seems happier. He's humming to himself as he drives.

The car struggles as we climb steeply and turn a hairpin bend. Mountains on one side, sweeping green valleys on the other.

'I'm sorry, Vivi,' Dad says suddenly. 'I know this wasn't how we planned our trip. I'll make sure we still do lots of things together, just us, don't worry.'

'That's OK,' I tell him.

'I wanted this road trip to be exactly like the ones me and Grandma would take together. But this whole journey has been showing me I need to let that go, and taking a little detour felt like embracing that. I can't control everything and Grandma would understand that.'

I nod. I can tell Dad doesn't want to let Grandma down in any way, just like me.

As we reach the top of the pass, I see patches of snow on the ground outside.

We all arrive at the campsite in Aspen several hours later. The place feels special to me because of my middle name, because of Grandma. We walk through a path of tall wildflowers and grasses to get to the site.

'It's just as I remember it,' says Dad happily.

Two flat dirt squares mark the ground for our tents. Seb and his mum get to work setting up theirs. A huge metal box stands to the side. I inspect the label on the box.

BEAR BOX

DO NOT KEEP FOOD OR
TOILETRIES IN YOUR TENT.
PLACE EVERYTHING IN THIS BOX.

'Are bears that common?' I ask, concerned.

'Oh yes,' says Dad. 'But don't worry, I have bear spray for when we go trekking.'

'Shouldn't we put it on now?' I ask.

'What?' asks Dad.

'The bear spray,' I reply. 'Can I put some on?'

He bites his lip. I can tell he's trying not to smile. 'You spray it at the bear, darling, not on yourself.'

'Oh,' I say, feeling my cheeks burn. 'I thought it was like mosquito spray.'

Seb bursts out laughing. Even his mum is smiling.

'We don't have bears in England!' I say, trying to defend myself, but I'm laughing too. 'Good job I asked before I used it,' I say, as I attach Bandit's lead and let him scamper around the campsite.

'That cheered me up,' says Seb, smiling at me.

For a split second I wonder if he's making fun of me but his dark eyes are kind and friendly.

Dad and I set up our tent under some aspen trees with their silvery trunks. Grandma loved trees. Every new place she visited she'd always talk about the trees there and give little snippets of information about them. That's how I know things like: the smallest tree is only one to six centimetres in height and called a dwarf willow, and that maple trees emit distress signals if under insect attack.

The aspen leaves shimmer and tremble in the breeze and their rippling leaves catch the sunlight. I breathe in deeply and feel Grandma in every flutter.

I feed Bandit some ferret food in a bowl, then put the rest of his food safely inside the bear box. After we set up the tent, I sit inside. Everything is tinted green from the sun shining through the fabric. I hear the gentle trickle of a nearby stream.

Through the entrance I catch sight of something, something with white, black and brown stripes running down its back. It's a chipmunk. It heads for Bandit's food bowl and stuffs pieces of Bandit's food into its cheeks. Bandit watches, then looks at me as if to say, *What on earth does this imposter think he's doing?*

'That's possibly the cutest little creature I've ever seen,' I say.

'Don't let Bandit hear you say that,' says Dad, putting his backpack in the tent porch.

I leave the tent to get a better look. I let go of Bandit's lead and Bandit heads over to the chipmunk. They sniff each other and Bandit pushes the bowl away from the chipmunk with his nose. I laugh and the chipmunk dashes away, only to return from a different direction. It soon becomes a game between them, until Bandit has eaten all of his food and the chipmunk scurries away in disappointment.

'I'm going to show Vivi the mountain walk I used to do with her grandma,' says Dad to Charlie.

'Have fun, you two,' she says. 'We'll go and buy firewood.'

I smile at him, grateful he's following through on his promise to hang out just the two of us.

We get back in the car and drive up to the base of some jagged mountains that have an alpine lake in front of them. The mountains appear and disappear as we turn every bend.

Once we arrive, we follow a steep path through a forest. Ravens caw overhead.

I look over at Dad and he's smiling.

'What is it?' I say.

'I was just thinking about Grandma. You know, even when we were on holidays, your grandma would practice singing. I'm sure she scared some people around here off with her singing exercises once.'

'Really?' I ask. 'Did she ever get nervous?'

'Oh, she was terrified before a show.'

'Really? Grandma? I can't imagine her being scared of anything.'

'That's because performing was so important to her that she was determined not to let her fear stop her. And I think after a while it got easier.'

'Did she ever make a mistake?' I ask. 'Did she ever mess up an audition?'

'I'm sure she did,' says Dad.

'But can you think of any times *specifically*?' I ask, desperate to hear that Grandma had failed sometimes too. 'Any parts she auditioned for and didn't get?'

'I've no idea sweetheart,' says Dad, pausing and resting with one hand against a tree trunk. 'She kept diaries. We can look through them together after our road trip?'

'Yes,' I say. 'Please.'

We walk the rest of the way in silence, listening to the birds and the rustling trees. I wrap my arms around myself. If Grandma was scared before auditions, then perhaps we are still alike.

By the time we reach the car park the sun's setting and the sky is filled with deep blues and bright pink clouds. A group of hikers are gathered at one end of the tarmac, pointing at a slope opposite.

'Do you want to see a bear?' a ranger asks.

'Yes!' I say. 'So long as it's from a distance.'

He laughs and points to a telescope further up the slope. There's a little line of people waiting.

Soon, it's my turn. As I press my eye against the telescope and spot a blur of brown, I laugh, feeling hopeful for the first time since the audition.

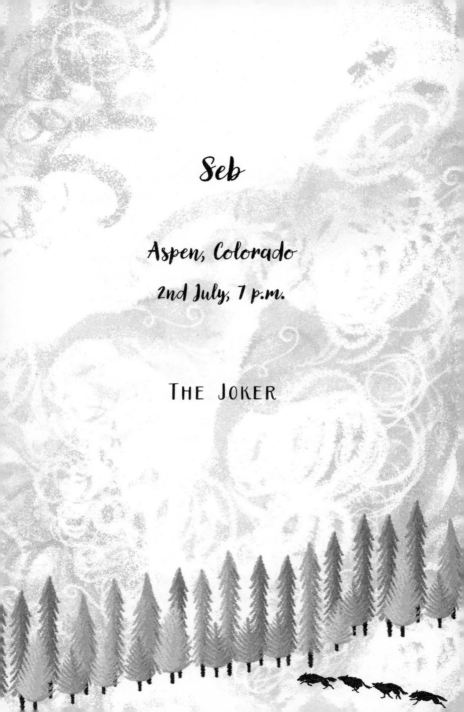

Seb

Aspen, Colorado
2nd July, 7 p.m.

THE JOKER

While Vivi and her dad are on a hike, Mom and I go to buy firewood from a log cabin campsite shop. The door has a note that says, 'Please knock', but when we do, no one answers.

'Can you check the board?' asks Mom. 'Maybe we're not allowed fires right now.'

Next to the cabin, there's a noticeboard that displays the level of forest fire threat. I hope we're allowed to have one. It might stop Vivi from worrying about the bears. Besides, it's freezing out here at night. Luckily the dial points to a low risk of fire spread today because it's rained recently.

We knock again and eventually the door opens and a woman comes out, apologising, saying she was out back. We return to the campsite with stacks of logs. We pile the wood inside the fire ring.

I sit under the tall, thin aspen trees. I am the calmest I've felt since the incident. The wind blows and the trees make a whispering, rustling sound.

In the Calamity Stoppers game our characters would recharge by sitting by a fire. We'd reset and heal if we'd been hurt by a monster or animal. We also had to stop if we pulled a joker. It was kind of like missing a turn. It was Clay's idea.

Maybe the card is telling me that if I'm going

to make it to Yellowstone I need to heal. I wasn't hit by any bullets, but the incident m de holes in different places in my life. I kept my eye on the gas gauge the whole way here; it's getting low. Tomorrow, we'll have to stop at a gas station. The thought fills my stomach with dread.

The sky darkens. 'Can I light the fire?' I ask.

'Sure, honey,' says Mom, reading inside the tent. 'The matches are here.'

I balance the logs on top of paper and kindling. Lighting a rolled-up newspaper, I stick it in to the centre and watch the flames lick and curl as they spread. The wood crackles and spits, catching.

Vivi and her dad return.

'You have a fire!' says Vivi, warming her hands on it. Bandit pokes his head above her fleece, sees the fire and immediately disappears again. 'So apparently my grandma loved to ride the gondolas up and down even in the summer when you couldn't ski, so I was thinking about doing that tomorrow.'

'No,' I say without thinking. We need to get to Yellowstone quickly; Clay needs me. 'I mean, I just, I'd really like to get to Yellowstone soon. Umm, before the rain comes.'

'The rain?' Josh asks.

'Yeah. There's supposed to be rain in a few

days.' I'm making this up because I know I sounded rude but I can't tell them the real reason we need to get there. Mum is frowning at me, but she looks more worried than angry.

'That's OK,' says Josh good-naturedly. 'How about we skip the gondola this time?'

Vivi scowls. 'Fine. But I'm not missing the hot swimming springs. They were her favourite place. It was one of Grandma's reasons for coming to Colorado every year. She said they were the "key to her vitality".' Vivi says the last few words in a dramatic old lady voice.

'Actually, I'd like to visit the springs too,' says Mom. She smiles understandingly at me. 'It will only set us back a few hours, Seb.'

Mom's twisting her necklace between her fingers, the way she does whenever she is worried about something, almost as if she's asking Dad to help. It was a gift from him. It's a ring and a charm that hang on a thin chain around her neck.

'I like your necklace,' says Vivi to Mom, noticing her twisting it too. As Mom turns it, the metal reflects the yellow fire.

'Thanks. It's very special,' says Mom, enclosing it in her hand.

'How far did you drive to get here?' I ask Vivi, trying to steer the conversation away from Dad.

'It was about eighteen hours of driving in total,

I think,' Vivi says. 'From Louisiana, through Texas, a tiny bit of Oklahoma, then into Colorado. And we only covered like a third of the country! I can't believe how big America is.'

'How long would it take to drive from one end of the UK to the other?' I ask.

Vivi's dad laughs. 'You can drive from Land's End in Cornwall to John o'Groats in Scotland in about fifteen hours. Those are the two furthest points.'

'That's cool,' I say. 'You must have seen the whole country.'

'Actually, we've never done it,' says Vivi. 'Maybe that should be our next trip, Dad?'

I check my phone for any news about Clay but there's nothing.

'Do you think a Pterodactyl is a dinosaur?' I ask Vivi, remembering my last conversation with Clay and wondering whose side she would have been on.

She tucks her hair behind her ears. 'I've never thought about it. I think it is though, yeah. It always is in films and stuff, isn't it?'

I smile. Clay had the popular opinion, that's for sure.

'You know what *I've* always wondered?' says Vivi. 'Why did the Tyrannosaurus rex have such tiny arms? What were they for?'

I laugh. 'I have no idea.'

As the stars start to come out, Vivi's dad begins to sing a song and after a few moments Vivi adds a harmony. She only sings softly, but it still makes her face light up and the flames dance in her eyes.

Vivi

Aspen, Colorado

3rd July, 8 a.m.

I open my eyes to heavy rain pattering on the canvas of the tent. Even though I went to bed happy, I wake up mad and angry at everything today. Unzipping the entrance, I peek out. It's soaking outside. *Great.*

I shiver. The cool air smells like eggs, toast and butter. One of the other families, parked in their RV, are cooking under awning. I'm starving.

Dad yawns and stretches. Once everyone's awake, we make a run for it through the rain to the Cadillac. I sit in the back next to Seb. Bandit springs onto his lap and curls up.

'He looks like a pretzel!' says Seb, his eyes lighting up.

I smile a bit at that.

'It's too wet to cook,' says Seb's mum.

'I think it's sandwiches for breakfast,' says Dad, pulling up his hood. 'I'll get the cool box.' He dashes into the rain to the bear box and gathers our food, then runs back. Dad passes us supplies from the front.

I make a peanut butter sandwich and take a bite. It's gooey and dry at the same time and sticks to the roof of my mouth.

Seb laughs at my unimpressed expression as I try and chew.

'You need the jelly,' he says. 'Here, let me make you one.'

He's so excited at the prospect that I let him. I don't have the heart to tell him Grandma made them for me when I was younger and I didn't like them then. I raise my eyebrows as he adds a slice of banana.

'Granted, the banana's a wild card,' he says, noticing. 'But I think you'll be surprised.'

I take a bite. It's not the most awful thing I've ever eaten.

'Good, right?' he asks.

I shrug. 'It's OK, I guess.'

He takes that as a win and smiles and tucks into his own sandwich. 'Me and Clay used to eat *waaay* too many of these.'

'Do you still want to go to the swimming pool springs in the rain?' asks Dad from the front.

I narrow my eyes. 'Definitely,' I say. 'We'll be wet anyway.'

'Clay loves swimming,' says Seb. 'Did your grandma like going to the beach as well as swimming in hot springs?'

I nod.

'Did she ever go on a jet ski?'

I shrug. I want him to stop asking me questions about her, it's just making me wish she was here. I can imagine her calling the landscape 'dramatic' in the rain and clutching her hands together theatrically as she turned around to take it all in.

'Did your grandma come here often?' Seb asks.

'Can we talk about something else?' I ask. The words come out meaner than I meant them to.

He looks taken aback. 'Sure. I need to go and pack up anyway.'

I feel a pang for snapping at him and watch Seb walk away in the rain, hunched over like my old pet hamster. It's not Seb's fault I'm feeling angry. I get out too. In the rain, everything feels unfair. I didn't have enough time with Grandma before she was gone.

Seb

Aspen, Colorado
3rd July, 9 a.m.

♥ THE JACK OF HEARTS ♥

I get it. She's just lost her grandma. Clay's still alive and I keep harping on about him. It's no wonder she doesn't want to talk to me about this stuff.

After packing up the tent we drive in our separate cars and we don't speak again until we're all swimming in the hot spring pool together. It looks like a normal outdoor swimming pool in the mountains, but it's super warm. Apparently the water comes from a deep spring. I've never been a confident swimmer and stay close to the side.

'Are you missing school to be here?' I ask Vivi. She nods.

'Me too,' I say.

'It's great, isn't it?' she says, but then she looks down into the water and I know we're thinking the same thing: that we'd choose going to school any day if it meant the incident hadn't happened.

'Vivi's going to play Alice in a theatre production of *Alice in Wonderland* when we get back,' says Vivi's dad, interrupting. He's smiling at her proudly.

I hadn't realised he'd been listening but I'm not surprised he heard, knowing my loud voice.

'Wow,' I say, turning to Vivi. 'You like acting? That's awesome.'

'I *love* acting,' she says, but there's something about her expression, the way she keeps her eyes on the water, that makes me think there's something she's not saying. A teenager jumps in next to us, splattering water everywhere. The lifeguard blows his whistle.

'What else do you like doing?' I ask.

'Playing football,' she says. 'Oh, I'm sorry, I mean *soccer*.'

I laugh and let go of the side to tread water.

'What kind of things are you into?' she asks.

'I like palaeontology and I play the guitar,' I say. 'And that role-playing game.'

I feel suddenly bare without the deck of cards in my pocket and grip the side of the pool. My heart quickens, but I remember what Christine told me to do. I count the number of people around me to slow my breaths. Eleven. I picture the eleven in the deck, the jack of hearts. It would be a good sign if I'd pulled the jack of hearts right now — *almost* a critical success.

'I wish I could play the guitar,' Vivi says, interrupting my thoughts. 'I like to sing, like my grandma.'

'Can you imagine her here?' I ask, gently, not wanting to upset her.

'Oh yes,' says Vivi. 'She'd be lying on one of those floats, sipping iced tea.'

I laugh. 'She sounds fun.'

'She was,' says Vivi. 'She was the best.'

After the hot spring, we pile back into our separate cars. Two hours later, I watch the dial of the gas gauge approach empty. My stomach turns. I've been dreading this moment since we set off.

'We'll have to stop at the next station,' says Mom. 'Are you sure you're going to be OK?'

I force a smile. 'I feel fine,' I say. 'I can do my breathing exercises.'

A few minutes later, we pull over into a huge gas station and restaurant complex. Vivi's car follows us in. So far, I'm feeling OK. Mom fills up the car. I count my breaths until I hear the click of the tank being full and am flooded with relief. I did it. I got through visiting a gas station. Even though it's a small thing, pride fills my chest. It means that I can make it to the rainbow pool.

'I'm going to grab some food inside,' says Josh, ambling over from their car. 'Want anything? Vivi's given me a long list.'

'I'd love a coffee.' Mom looks at me, tipping her head to the side. 'How are you doing, honey?'

'I feel great,' I say, and I do. I grin at her. 'You can go in if you want. Would you get me a snack?'

She laughs. 'OK then.' She pulls the car over to the parking area and heads inside with Josh.

I wait outside the car with Vivi. I ask her about the play she'll be in — it's all about a little girl who falls down a rabbit hole. We're talking, but I can feel my chest getting tighter and tighter, until I can't make any words come out.

What if there's another robbery?

I imagine the shots ringing out, the silence and then the screaming. My head swims and I bend over.

'Are you OK?' asks Vivi.

I'm sweating. I can't speak. All I can do is gulp down air.

Vivi kneels beside me. 'Should I get your mom?'

I shake my head. I don't want Vivi to leave and then to be alone here.

'This is what I do before I go onstage,' she says. 'Breathe with me. In one, two, three. Out two, three.'

I try and say that's what my therapist told me to do too, but the words get stuck at the back of my throat. I focus on my breathing instead. It's easier with her counting. 'Are people staring?' I manage to ask.

'No one can see you,' she says. Her voice is kind.

I sit down and hug my head to my knees, trying to focus on her counting.

After a few minutes, the pounding in my chest subsides.

We sit in the parking lot on the cement, leaning against the car, away from the gas station.

'You were there at the shooting, weren't you?' she says.

I nod.

'I can't imagine how awful that must have been,' she says. 'You should give Bandit a hug. It helps, honestly. Even though he's a bit smelly.'

I laugh and pet the ferret. 'Did you know elephants show sadness when an elephant in their family dies?'

'I didn't,' says Vivi.

'Where are they?' I hear Mom's voice and stand up.

'Please don't say anything about . . . you know,' I ask Vivi. I'm so close to saving Clay at Yellowstone I can't risk Mom wanting to take me home.

'I won't,' she says and she smiles at me.

'Look what I found in there!' says Vivi's dad as he throws something to Vivi.

'A Hacky Sack!' says Vivi and she kicks it over to me.

I balance it on my trainer before kicking it in the air and sending it back towards her.

She knees it over towards me. Her dad intercepts it and joins in, laughing. Mom watches us, grinning.

If it wasn't for the ringing in my ears, it's almost as if the anxiety attack never happened.

Vivi

Jackson Hole, Wyoming
3rd July, 1.25 p.m.

Seb hadn't struck me as the kind of person who has anxiety attacks. He's loud and seems confident. He always looks cheerful and relaxed.

So when I saw him crouching down in the car park, I didn't know what was going on. For a split second, I wondered if he was having a heart attack. Then I wondered if it was some kind of joke.

But when he lifted his head and I saw the panic in his eyes, I knew that it was real. At first, I didn't know what to do except comfort him, but then I remembered one of the exercises we do in drama — a counting your breaths one — and I led him through it.

It helped him feel a tiny bit better, I think. I hope so.

I didn't think about the fact that he'd been there, when the shooting was actually happening, and how terrifying that must have been. No wonder he was so quiet the first time we met at the memorial.

After the mountains in Colorado, I can't believe how flat the land is on the drive through Wyoming to Yellowstone. It goes on and on, just a straight road with vast plains and grass prairie around it. We pass ranches with horses and cows. The sky is big and wide.

Dad taps his fingers against the steering wheel in time to a country song on the radio. I smile at him. He catches me looking at him.

'What?' he asks, glancing at me. 'Why are you looking at me like that?'

I raise my eyebrows at him. 'It's just nice to see you so happy,' I say.

'Thanks, bean,' he says, reaching over and ruffling my hair. 'This is turning out to be quite a trip.'

The flat drive goes on for so long that I begin to wonder if there really is a volcano here. It seems so unlikely. Then, all of a sudden, I see the ridge of misty mountains in the distance, jutting out of the landscape like a row of teeth.

The rain starts again and the windscreen wipers squeak as they go back and forth. I feel gusts of wind pushing up against the car. After thirty minutes we reach the mountains. Once we're in them, we're surrounded by tree-covered slopes and gushing rivers.

The car starts making a rattling noise.

'Should we be worried?' I ask.

'Cormac is doing just fine,' Dad says. 'Look!'

A herd of elk are grazing next to us. Dad pulls over and I lean out the window to watch them.

The rain is now a drizzle. Charlie parks behind us and Seb leans out the window too. He points at a huge elk standing at the edge of the group and then mimes having antlers.

I laugh.

We drive on. An hour later we stop and get food in a town called Jackson Hole.

I've been dying to try out the new trainers that Grandma got me but so far everywhere has been too muddy. This town is all roads and pavements. I slide them on. They hug my feet perfectly with each step.

'Oh my gosh,' I say. 'These are the most amazing things I've ever worn.'

As we walk, I catch my reflection in the shop windows and smile.

'Nice sneakers,' says Seb, as we meet up with them at the corner.

'Thanks,' I say.

In the town square there are big arches made out of thousands of elk antlers.

'Do they have to kill the elk to get the antlers?' I ask, worried.

Dad shakes his head. 'They shed them every year.'

We pass a theatre.

'I wonder if they'd let us look inside?' asks Dad.

'It's closed,' I say firmly, hoping he won't look any closer to double-check.

Just thinking about the theatre makes my skin crawl. I have a faint memory of the excitement and anticipation I used to feel when the lights went out and I was about to perform, but it's drowned out by the sense of humiliation. I can't get the failed audition out of my head.

Will I ever be able to perform again?

After lunch, we all walk along Snake River. It's wide with a flat bed of pebbles either side and then forest. I carefully step on the dry, clean stones in my new trainers. A cloud of midges follows above my head and I swat them away.

Our parents walk slowly behind Seb and me, laughing and chatting.

'Yellowstone's only three hours away from here,' says Seb eagerly. 'We're almost there.'

We pause and perch on a rock, waiting for our parents to catch up.

'Why are you in such a rush to get there anyway?' I ask.

To my surprise, his expression changes.

'You'll think it's stupid,' he says quietly.

'It can't be as stupid as thinking you *wear* bear spray,' I say.

He laughs. 'OK then.' He takes a deep breath. 'There's a special rainbow pool at Yellowstone — I don't know exactly where. It was Clay's idea to go there for the finale of our game. We would have had to find it and agree on a wish to make there together. And then it would come true.'

I listen while he talks. I don't laugh.

'If I can just get there and make this wish,' he finishes, 'I know it will help Clay. I can't explain why, but I do.'

'I get it,' I say, thinking about Grandma and the audition and how it felt as if she was there in a way. There are some things you just know.

Seb hesitates. 'I was wondering . . .' he says. But before he can finish, Bandit scampers on ahead, pulling on the lead, and I chase after him.

Seb bends and picks up some driftwood. It's sun-bleached and smooth, and looks kind of like a wand. 'These would make great props for our next campaign,' he says, collecting them as we walk.

'I wonder if Bandit would fetch?' I ask, and toss a twig away.

Bandit dashes after it but loses interest once it has landed.

'He's a good pet,' says Seb.

'My grandma loved him a lot. I've seen a

picture of them with matching pink scarves tied over their heads.'

'Your grandma wore a pink scarf?' he asks, turning to me, eyes wide.

'Her signature scarf, she called it. She always wore it.'

He nods slowly.

On the way back to the car we see a lone moose swimming across the river. Its big head and huge flattened antlers stick up above the water. Its face is long with big brown eyes and a velvety muzzle. The antlers must be about six feet long.

I'm so distracted by the moose I don't realise I've stepped in mud.

'No!' I say, wiping my new trainers in the grass, trying to get the mud off.

Dad and Charlie have caught us up. 'Listen, between us, I don't like the sound Cormac was making earlier,' Dad says. 'I think we should find someone in town to take a look at it. We can ride with Charlie and Seb the rest of the way.'

Most of the mud has come off the sides of the trainers and I give up trying to rub it off the tread. It will have to do for now. I can wipe them fully clean later.

'OK,' I reply to Dad, feeling surprisingly happy about sharing a car with Seb and his mum. Ever since his anxiety attack, I've felt protective of him. This is really hard for him too. 'Is there room for our bags?'

'I'll see what I can fit,' says Dad.

After we stuff our tent and Bandit's cage in the back of Seb's car, we drop Cormac the Cadillac off at a mechanic's and all pile into the one car. Seb and I are squished together in the back. Bandit curls up between us and goes to sleep.

'Look,' says Seb. 'He's curled up in the shape of a heart.'

Bandit's whiskers twitch as he dreams.

Seb

Yellowstone National Park, Wyoming

3rd July, 3.25 p.m.

♥ THE FIVE OF HEARTS ♥

I think I met Vivi's grandma before she died. I think she was the elegant old lady with the pink scarf, the one who wanted a cold can of lemonade.

But I don't know if I should tell Vivi. Will it make her upset?

I also couldn't find a way to tell Vivi that I need her to make the wish with me at the pool. When I told her about the rainbow pool all she said was, 'I get it.' But I don't know if she really *does* get it. I guess I'm scared she'll say no. What will I do then?

If we were playing Calamity Stoppers, I'd pick a card to determine how likely it is that she would say yes. I flip over the top card from my deck now. The five of hearts. It could still go either way.

We pull into a restaurant for lunch and while Vivi and her dad walk inside, Mom stops me.

'I've just heard from Clay's dad,' she says.

My jaw tightens. 'How's Clay?'

'He's having his operation tomorrow morning. They think he has a really good chance of making a full recovery. But we just need to wait and see now.'

'Could I see him?' I ask. 'If we were at home?'

Mom shakes her head. 'He still can't have visitors. His heartbeat has to be kept very stable.'

I nod. If his operation is tomorrow, then I

have to reach the rainbow pool before then to give Clay the *best* chance of being OK.

Three hours later we hit a queue of cars waiting to enter Yellowstone. My stomach's full of butterflies. We're FINALLY here!

'When there's a traffic jam it's usually because an animal, like a grizzly bear or wolf, is in the road,' says Mom.

We turn a corner and see the reason: a herd of bison crossing the road. They're huge and swing their big heads from side to side as they walk. I lean out and take a picture to show Clay.

When the bison have finally crossed, the cars continue onwards and we're soon past the entrance. I examine the map in the leaflet we were given and offer directions to Mom.

'Did you know that some of the pools are acidic? They contain naturally occurring chemicals. A few years ago someone fell into one of the pools and they dissolved completely,' I say, reading from the leaflet.

'Oh my gosh, that's terrible!' says Vivi. 'Were people watching?'

'Must have been,' I say. 'Otherwise how would they know?'

'Better stay a safe distance from those pools then,' says Vivi's dad, jokingly.

'As if I'd go *anywhere* near a hot acidic pool,' says Vivi. She nods at the leaflet. 'Can I look when you're done?' I hand it to her.

'The Morning Glory pool is right here,' I say, pointing at a car park up ahead. 'Past Old Faithful.' I remember from our school project that Old Faithful is a geyser that erupts with steaming water on average every seventy-two minutes.

'The leaflet says it's known as "Fading Glory" now because early visitors threw trash in it which has disrupted the vents,' says Vivi, flicking through it. 'That's so sad.'

I wonder if that's a sign it's not the rainbow pool Clay meant for us to go to.

As soon as we step out of the car, I smell sulphur. The air is cool and I slip on my raincoat.

'I thought volcanos were supposed to be hot,' says Vivi, shivering.

We cross the car park and come to a clearing and it's as if we've stepped onto another planet. The ground is a chalky white with bands of unexpected colours: yellows, rust-reds and bronzes. Deep craters filled with bright green and blue pools dot the landscape. Strange rock formations jut out around a small geyser to the side. Huge plumes of steam billow out of vents and holes.

'Old Faithful's about to erupt!' says Mom. 'Look!' We rush over to where a crowd of people are gathering.

Almost as soon as we arrive a tall jet of water erupts from the ground high into the sky. I wish I could float on the top of it. It roars loudly.

My body tingles all over with the anticipation of being so close to the rainbow pool and so close to saving Clay. I can't let anything screw this up. I glance at Vivi, who is gazing at the geyser, and hope she'll say yes.

Vivi

Yellowstone

3rd July, 4.40 p.m.

Seb taps me on the shoulder and points silently at something behind me. I spin around to look where he's pointing.

Dad and his mum are holding hands. Just for a moment, then they let go, but they're smiling. They don't see us notice.

Seb rolls his eyes at them but he's grinning. I smile too. Grandma would be pleased that Dad's happy. Who knows, maybe we'll do this trip every year too, like him and Grandma did. She was always talking about creating family traditions. I wouldn't mind coming back here every year.

'Let's take a photo in front of the erupting geyser,' says Dad, walking up to me. The landscape looks like something you'd find on Mars and I imagine I'm in a movie about aliens and strike a courageous pose, one hand on my hip, one hand in the air, like I'm the first person to discover them.

Dad laughs and clicks away.

Behind Dad, there's a baby facing outwards in a sling, smiling and waving at everyone.

My phone pings. I haven't had mobile data or even phone reception for ages. It's my friend Sarah. She was auditioning for a part in *Alice in Wonderland* too.

Guess what? I've been offered the part of Alice!

My stomach drops and I'm tinged with jealousy. Rita Ali, the famous director, will never even know I exist, let alone watch my acting. I really thought it would be my big break.

The geyser finishes erupting and everyone claps. I can't bring myself to join in with them, and my arms stay heavy by my sides. More than anything else, I feel the weight of my lie. There's really no way out of it now. Soon everyone will know that Sarah is playing the part of Alice and that I lied. What will I say to Dad?

Seb

Upper Geyser Basin, Yellowstone

3rd July, 5 p.m.

 THE ACE OF HEARTS

After the geyser has finished erupting, we walk on boards above the thermal hot springs and bubbling mud. There are signs telling people to stay on the boardwalks. The others keep stopping at every geyser to read about them.

'Oh, this one's going to erupt soon, let's wait for it,' says Mom.

'I'm going to check out the other pools while you wait,' I say and leave them staring into bubbling water. Vivi looks distracted and worried, but I don't have time to see what's wrong. I have to get to the rainbow pool. Of course, the Morning Glory pool is the furthest one away, right at the end of the boardwalk.

But when I get to the end, my heart sinks. I know instantly that this isn't the one. I pull out the handbook to check anyway. This pool's tiny and Clay wrote that the rainbow one was huge. And the colours aren't right. The middle isn't a brilliant blue but a dull green. The outer rims of it are yellow and it's rust-coloured at the edges. It's not really rainbow-coloured at all. I chew my lip.

'It's the wrong one,' I say to myself, deflated. My hands close around the cards in my pocket and I pull one out. The ace of hearts. A critical fail!

'Seb!' calls Mom, catching up to me. 'There you are! You know there's life in these pools?

Isn't that incredible? I just read that heat-loving microbes were discovered in them.'

She's so excited I don't have the heart to tell her I already knew that from my school project.

Josh looks at his watch. 'We need to check in to our campsite before it gets too late. Then we should think about dinner.' The whole way here he's been telling us he is looking forward to barbecuing. He picked up an ice chest and food supplies in Jackson Hole.

We pile back into the car. I examine all the road signs. We pass one that says Grand Prismatic Spring. It must be the rainbow pool.

'I think that's the one,' I say. My voice gets louder. 'THAT'S THE POOL I WANT TO SEE. Stop!'

Vivi smiles at me understandingly. Maybe she does get it after all. It's a positive sign that she'll say yes.

'Let's go in the morning,' says Mom, yawning.

'Yeah, it's been a long day,' says Josh. 'We've all been up since five.'

I glare at him. This was supposed to be my trip with Mom and the only reason we were up at five is so he could go to his stupid hot spring swimming pool. I catch myself; it's not his fault Clay's in hospital.

By the time we've set up our tents it's dark and Vivi's dad has already lit the fire to barbecue.

Mom has been rummaging in the car. 'Has anyone seen my necklace?' she calls. 'I took it off to go swimming in the hot springs earlier. I left it in the cup holder.'

'No, sorry,' says Vivi. She's perched in a camp chair stoking Bandit on her lap.

'I'll help you look in the car,' says Dad. 'It's probably just fallen under a seat.'

I pass them to go to the restrooms. When I come back, they're still at the car. They don't hear me come up. Mom's talking in a hushed voice. She sounds upset.

'But it was right here! Someone must have moved it.'

'I don't see how,' says Josh. 'Maybe you put it somewhere else?'

'I know where I put it,' says Mom. 'Is there any chance Vivi could have taken it to have a look at? She said she liked it earlier.'

'That doesn't mean she wanted to steal it!' whispers Josh heatedly.

I stand in the darkness, unsure of what to do. I wasn't trying to eavesdrop.

'I didn't say she stole it,' Mom snaps.

'I think you probably just lost it,' says Josh.

'I wouldn't lose this necklace,' Mom says.

'Well can you search a bit harder before you start accusing my daughter?'

Even in the dark, I can tell they're glaring at each other.

'You know,' says Mom, and I can tell she's really angry now, 'this whole necklace thing has got me thinking that I don't really know much about you at all, do I? We've been brought together by this tragedy but that's all we have in common.'

'Fine,' Josh says. 'Maybe tomorrow we should drive back to our separate cars.'

'Fine by me,' says Mom coolly. She storms away, straight past me.

I wave at her and she jumps when she sees me.

'What are you doing there?' she asks.

'I was just on my way back from the restroom,' I say. 'Mom? I really want to go to that pool tomorrow.'

'Maybe me and you can go together. We'll have to see,' says Mom and she disappears into the tent to keep searching for the necklace, leaving me standing in the darkness.

I learnt from our school project that Old Faithful shoots water up into the air because pressure builds below the ground until it's too much and the water is forced through the surface.

That's exactly how I feel at this moment. I'm so close to making the wish. I can't fail now.

Vivi

Campsite, Yellowstone

3rd July, 11 p.m.

I toss and turn on the airbed, unable to sleep. Earlier, Dad had asked me if I'd moved Charlie's necklace. When I'd said 'no', Dad said that was fine, he knows I'm not a liar.

But he doesn't realise that I *am* a liar and everyone will find out soon enough. I pull my sleeping bag over my head.

I wrap my arms around my body. I'm pretty sure I've forgotten to put a bit of Bandit's ferret food in the bear box. Images of a bear hunting around the tent for Bandit's food keep flashing through my mind. *Perfect.* There's no way I'll ever be able to sleep now. I grab my torch and carefully lift Bandit's food out of my bag so as not to wake Dad.

I unzip the tent and climb out with Bandit tucked under my arm. I carry the bag to the bear box, taking the torch.

There's a person right outside the tent! I jump. My heart thumps.

'Don't scream! It's me,' whispers Seb.

'What are you doing?' I hiss.

'I was going to ask you something,' he says.

'I didn't take your mum's stupid necklace,' I say.

'I know,' whispers Seb. 'But it's not that. Let's sit around the fire for a second.'

We both sit down around the glowing embers. Crickets and bugs sound around us.

'Why is your mum so worried about the necklace, anyway?' I ask, since it doesn't seem like Seb is going to speak any time soon.

'It's not just any old necklace,' says Seb. 'My dad gave her the ring on it.' He goes quiet and sighs. 'Before he died. She wears it every day.'

My stomach drops. I had no idea. 'I'm sorry. I didn't realise,' I say. I think how sad I would be if I lost Grandma's earrings. 'That makes sense now. I wish I could help her find it.'

'Me too.'

'What are we going to do about our parents?' I ask. 'They were so happy earlier. And now they're fighting.'

'I don't know,' says Seb. 'My mom won't be happy until she finds that necklace.' He puts a log on the embers. It catches. I warm my hands on the flames.

Seb pokes the log with a long stick over and over again.

The fire is making me sleepy and I yawn.

'I need to go back to bed soon,' I say.

'Wait,' says Seb suddenly. He meets my eyes for a second and then drops his gaze. 'You know that rainbow pool and the wish I told you about?'

I nod.

'In the game, the rules state that two or more people must make the same wish at the same time for it to come true . . .' He trails off and bites his lip.

'OK,' I say, not sure where Seb is going with this.

'So,' continues Seb, 'I need someone to make the wish with me.'

I squint at him through the darkness. 'Are you asking me to make the wish with you?'

'Yes!' he says, sounding relieved. His body relaxes and he throws the stick into the flames.

'I don't see why not,' I say, stroking Bandit's soft nose.

'Phew,' says Seb. 'I wasn't sure you'd want to do it.'

'Really? Why?' I ask, not sure if I should be offended. I thought we'd become friends.

'You weren't too happy about getting your sneakers dirty yesterday, and all the pools look pretty muddy in the pictures . . .'

'Oh!' I say. I laugh. 'I don't care about getting muddy usually. But those shoes were a present from Grandma. I didn't want to ruin them. Did you think I was super fussy?'

'Maybe a bit,' says Seb, looking embarrassed. 'Will you still make the wish with me?'

'Of course,' I say, standing up to go to bed. 'We can go first thing tomorrow.'

'No,' Seb whispers urgently. 'We need to go now.'

'*Now* now?' I ask. 'Like, in the dark?'

'Yes! My mom and your dad say we need to split up in the morning and I need you with me to complete the wish.'

He looks desperate.

'Do you definitely know where the pool is?' I say. 'You can go to prison for wandering off the paths — I read the leaflet. Or worse. Die.'

'I know where it is. I saw the sign for it earlier. We just need to go back along the road a bit and then there will be boardwalks to follow when we get closer,' says Seb.

'You sure?' I ask. 'I don't want to go anywhere near those boiling pools.'

'Yep.'

'But isn't it too dangerous in the dark with the animals around?' I ask, staring into the blackness around us.

'I've got two torches.' His face is illuminated by the fire. He looks alert. 'And don't worry about the animals, we'll just be on the road for most of it. We won't actually be in their territory. We can get to the pool and get back in a few hours. Our parents won't even know that we were gone.'

I think about it. It's not like I'll be able to sleep right now anyway. I'll be worried about Dad after his argument with Seb's mum, worried about the true cast of *Alice in Wonderland* being revealed soon, worried about Seb going off by himself.

And there's something else, something important. Clay tried to save Grandma in the petrol station. I know she'd want me to do everything I can to save him.

'I'll come with you,' I say. 'But it's freezing, so let me get more layers.'

'Do you have to?' asks Seb. 'You might wake your dad up going back in there.'

'If there's one thing Grandma taught me, it's always dress properly for the weather,' I say. 'Besides, what if Bandit gets cold? I need to bring a blanket for him. I'll be quiet, promise.'

Inside the tent, Dad is still sleeping soundly, snoring. I inch my way across my sleeping bag towards my backpack and quietly stuff it full of all the warm clothes I have. Dad stirs and I freeze.

He rolls over and I hold my breath.

'What time is it?' Dad's sleepy voice asks.

'I think it's the middle of the night,' I say, trying to sound half-asleep too. 'I'm just putting on an extra layer.'

'OK, bean.'

I wait until his breathing is rhythmic again and grab my hat, then climb out of the tent, hoping that he stays fast asleep the whole time we're gone. I don't want him to worry.

Outside, the air is wet and dewy. I wrap Bandit up in a blanket and carry him in my arms. Seb waves at me from by the fire. 'I thought you'd fallen asleep,' he says.

I smile. 'I had to make sure Dad didn't wake up.'

Before we leave our camp, we stop at the bear box. I pack some snacks and Bandit's ferret food and find a flask full of hot chocolate that's still warm. I'm ready now.

Seb

Midway Geyser Basin, Yellowstone

3rd July, 11.30 p.m.

♥ EIGHT OF HEARTS ♥

I can't believe that after all this time I'm finally going to make it to the rainbow pool. I pull a card from the deck and shine the torch on the face of it. The eight of hearts. It's a good omen.

Adrenaline shoots around my body. I don't feel tired AT ALL. I lead Vivi down to the path and to the road, retracing the route we drove earlier. I keep looking back at the tents, silhouetted in the darkness. But there's no shine of flashlights, no call for us. My eyes adjust to the night.

The stars above are bright and twinkling.

Geysers rumble in the distance. The trees rustle and whisper.

'Are you sure you know the way?' whispers Vivi after a while.

I nod. 'There's a sign somewhere here.' I shine the torch around as we walk.

Finally, the flashlight hits the sign and it gleams back at us. 'There. Look!' I say excitedly. It points to a smaller road we haven't been along yet. 'It's just down there.'

'Great!' she says.

We walk in silence. It seems strange to disturb the quietness of the night.

'I wish I could stay on this trip for ever,' says Vivi, breaking it.

'How come?' I ask.

Through the darkness I can just see her shrug.

There is dense forest on either side of the road. It looks scary. Being on the road I feel safe though, distanced from it.

The truth is I'm nervous about getting to this pool. What if, after everything, it doesn't work?'

'What if it's not enough?' I say out loud without thinking.

Vivi glances at me. 'All you can do is try, right?' Her voice is shaky and scared.

From the moonlight, I spot a shadow on the road ahead. An animal crossing. I put my hand out and stop Vivi.

'What is that?' she asks. 'A mountain lion?'

The animal stops and looks straight at us. Then it alters its path and starts heading in our direction, walking on all fours until it stops about twenty yards away.

It's bigger than I first thought. It has a bulky body but no antlers or pointy ears like an elk and it's too round for a big cat. Maybe a coyote? No, it's *waaaay* too big. My heart pounds. It rears up on its back legs and is about eight foot tall. It's definitely not a coyote.

It's a bear.

A huge grizzly bear, making a low growling sound.

Watching us.

Vivi

Midway Geyser Basin, Yellowstone

4th July, 12.05 a.m.

'Do you have the bear spray?' I whisper. I can't believe that I didn't think to bring it myself.

Bandit scurries from my arms to the hood of my jacket. Seb reaches slowly into his pocket. Terror ripples through my body. How big the bear is takes my breath away — and how strong and powerful and wild.

I can't take my eyes off it. Even its paw must be four times the size of my hand. One swipe and I'd be knocked out cold.

We shouldn't be here. We made a bad decision. There are no fences here. *All* of this place is bear territory. I saw the bison crossing the road yesterday; I know that there's nothing to stop the animals coming onto the road.

Everything inside me is screaming at myself to run back to the camp, back to Dad. But it's too late now. I know that bears can run very fast. The bear lowers itself to all fours and pats the ground with its paw aggressively.

'Slowly back away,' Seb says to me in a low voice. The spray is in his hand now.

The bear has a dished face, rounded ears, and a large shoulder hump. It opens its mouth, and sharp, pointy teeth glimmer in the moonlight. The bear looks angry, upset that we're in its home.

I try and slowly back away, half-frozen with fear. This doesn't feel like it's really happening.

I could be dreaming. But then the bear growls and I know it's real.

'It's not working,' I hiss at Seb.

'Keep moving backwards,' says Seb. 'Slowly.'

All of a sudden, the bear charges straight towards us.

'Stand your ground. Stand your ground!' Seb shouts at me. 'Stay next to me!'

I stay, even though everything is telling my body to run. Seb grips the bear spray with both hands, holding it in front of him. Bandit's sharp little claws are tearing into my back. He's hissing. At least I think that the hissing sound is coming from him. I'm not completely sure. I didn't even know a ferret could hiss like a snake. My legs are propelling me backwards. The bear is bounding towards us.

'Don't run!' Seb screams at me.

I try to stop, to stand my ground, but my legs aren't listening to my brain.

And the bear is getting closer and closer.

Seb

Midway Geyser Basin, Yellowstone

4th July, 12.06 a.m.

 THE TWO OF HEARTS

You're supposed to stay at least a hundred yards from a bear. They have four-inch claws. You should never run as they're likely to chase you. If a bear charges, you need to stand your ground and use bear spray.

These are the things I know.

The things I don't know are how difficult it is to take the safety latch off bear spray with shaking hands. And how hard it *really* is to stand your ground with a bear charging at you.

Steadying my hands, I rip the safety latch away. I yell and squeeze the trigger. It creates a misty cloud in front of me. I aim it straight ahead and slightly tilted down, so the bear will have to come through the mist to reach us. I spray until there's nothing left.

Another thing I know: If bear spray doesn't work, you should lie down and play dead.

Vivi turns and runs.

'Don't run!' I scream. 'Please stop, Vivi.'

Running is the worst thing you could do. I hold my breath to see if the bear has noticed her but it's reached the cloud of bear spray and stumbled, thrashing its head from side to side.

At this point you're supposed to back away, slowly. I try but I know I'm moving too quickly. The bear clears its vision and looks for me again. And as it does, for a split second it meets my eyes. I quickly look away — eye contact can be seen as a threat.

The bear shakes its head. I can feel it sensing me again. I hold my breath. The bear steps forward towards me. Adrenaline courses through my body.

Then the bear bows its head and turns away with a growl. My breaths are short and raspy. The bear is still in the road. I watch the round silhouette of its back slowly walking away, towards the forest.

I duck down a ridge, off the road, and then I'm running, dodging the trees, trying to put as much distance between me and the bear as possible.

'Vivi?' I whisper. 'Vivi?' I say a bit louder. *Where is she? Where did she go?*

Suddenly I'm completely surrounded by trees. I spin around and trip over a root and thud to the ground. My torch goes flying and my deck of cards spills out of my pocket. I grab the torch and scramble to pick them up. I think I have all of them. The two of hearts catches the light. I shove the cards back into my pocket and stand on shaky legs.

I need to stop moving and listen.

At the same time as listening, I clap every so often. I don't want to surprise another bear. Silvery light from the moon streams in between the narrow tree trunks. I whip my head around and around, searching for Vivi.

I see movement through the trees and my heart jumps — another bear? But then I make out antlers. A deer lifts its head and then scatters away as soon as it sees me.

I try and spot the road but all I can see are tree trunks and undergrowth. I'm completely alone, lost in the forest.

Vivi

Midway Geyser Basin, Yellowstone

4th July, 12.09 a.m.

I ran. I couldn't help it. The bear was getting closer and closer. I looked back as I sprinted off and saw Seb using the bear spray. It seemed like it was working. Even so, I couldn't get my legs to stop. My whole body was screaming at me to get as far away as possible.

But now I don't know where Seb is. I thought he would run straight after me. I gingerly step back towards where I think the road is. But it's not there.

'Seb?' I whisper. 'Seb!' A bit louder this time. I spin around. I'm in a thick cluster of pines. It's darker than on the road and strange animal calls and bird screeches fill the air.

Where is the road?

I peel Bandit off my neck and cup him in front of me. 'Are you OK, Bandit?' I ask. He pokes his nose under the opening to the sleeve on my wrist and squeezes into my jacket. I wish I could hide away like that too.

A tree rustles and I jump. 'Seb?'

Shadows twitch, but there's no sign of him. Panic begins to rise. What if the bear got Seb? He could be hurt, crushed or bleeding somewhere. I cover my mouth with my hand. How could I have run?

Maybe I'll be able to see more up a tree? Do bears climb trees?

I shine the torch over the trunks. There's a

bent one that would be easy to climb but I'm not sure it's safe. The branches don't look very sturdy.

Then, behind it, I spot the reflection of the moon glittering on the swaying leaves of an aspen tree. I breathe a sigh of relief. Grandma's favourite tree.

'I'm going to have to zip you up in my pocket, just for a second,' I tell Bandit. 'I can't lose you out here.' I leave an inch of zipper open so that he can breathe and he immediately pushes his nose out and sniffs.

'Hold on tight,' I say.

I place the torch between my teeth and swing the blanket in my backpack over the strongest-looking branch above me. Then I grab on to each end of the blanket and walk my legs up the trunk, pulling myself up by the blanket until I can grasp the branch.

I repeat the process three times until I'm as high as I can go. It should be high enough to get a good view of the area. I'm out of breath so I let myself take a short break, sitting on a branch with my legs on either side of it, facing the tree, and gripping the trunk. I can wrap my whole arm around the tree easily.

I let Bandit out of my pocket. He peeks out and looks down towards the ground, then up at me as if I'm mad. 'I'm sorry,' I say to him. 'I didn't know what else to do! I need to try and see where Seb is. I'm pretty sure bears don't climb aspen trees, though. So we're safe for now.'

Bandit nuzzles into my neck, like a scarf.

But when I shine the torch around me, I can hardly see any more from up here than I could from the ground. We're surrounded by trees. The slopes opposite are covered too.

'Seb!' I shout. I shine the torch on the ground below me, then all around in a circle. Maybe he'll see it even if he can't hear me.

Unless he's being eaten by the bear and I've just left him there to die.

What have I done?

Seb was using the bear spray.

I have to believe it worked.

I scour my surroundings once more. In the distance, plumes of steam rise in the moonlight. I can't believe I'm lost in this alien landscape.

That's when I notice markings on the bark of the trunk next to me. Five long, deep scratches. There's only one thing that could have made them.

Trust me to climb a bear's favourite tree.

Seb

Midway Geyser Basin, Yellowstone
4th July, 12.33 a.m.

♥ THE FOUR OF HEARTS ♥

You'd think having a loud voice would come in handy during moments like this. I scream as loud as I can.

'VIVI!' I face a different direction and yell, 'HELP! IS THERE ANYONE OUT THERE?'

At the very least, I hope I've scared away the wild animals.

'VIVI!' I shout again. 'WHERE ARE YOU?' How could I lose her that quickly?

The wind whips up and dark clouds cover the sky. Sudden storms can appear at any time here in Yellowstone. I lose the only bit of natural light I had.

'VIVI!'

The wind gets stronger and stronger, drowning out my shouts.

I'm lost in the trees. What do I do? What if I'm moving further and further away from Vivi and the road?

This is all just like something that would happen in our game. I let my hands close around the deck of cards. Should I keep moving and look for Vivi? Or stay here in case she's wandering around and looking for me? If it's a high card I move, if it's a low card I stay put.

I flip over the top card. The four of hearts. That's decided. I stay put.

I search for somewhere to shelter from the

wind. Not too far ahead is the looming shape of a cliff. Thunder rumbles in the distance.

I hope Vivi is close by and OK. I'm the whole reason she's out here. I'll see her soon. I have to.

Vivi

Midway Geyser Basin, Yellowstone

4th July, 1 a.m.

I shine the torch in the branches around me. There's no bear up here. At least, not yet. I hope with all my might that one doesn't climb up later.

The wind picks up and the branches around me bend and creak. I shriek, scared they might completely snap off. This was supposed to be my safe spot. I was even starting to think about waiting up here until it gets light and I could find Seb again. There can't be that many hours until daylight, can there? It feels as if we've been out here for ages already. Maybe Dad's already searching for us.

That's when I realise. If anything happens to me, Dad will have nobody.

Thunder rumbles in the distance. A storm is moving this way.

A huge branch breaks loose from the tree next to me and is whipped straight towards me by the wind. I duck to avoid the branch and shield Bandit, who's still curled up and around my neck, almost losing my balance and toppling out of the tree. I steady myself and hang on tightly.

The tree sways back and forth. I just want to be in my tent, warm and cosy. Actually, forget the tent; I want a shower, a warm towel and my fluffy slippers. I want my comfy bed and the drop of lavender that Grandma would put on my pillow before I went to sleep. I want to go home.

'Should we get down?' I whisper to Bandit.

But then the lightning starts and I'm too scared to move. It cracks through the sky in bursts of pink, branching towards the ground. It touches the tops of trees in the distance.

One of the trees is smouldering and I realise the lightning has caught it on fire. I duck and hide my face with my hand, but can't resist peeking through my fingers to look.

The wind rages around me. My hat flies off. Lightning bolts through the sky, closer this time. Thunder booms above me. The storm is moving closer — I have to get down. I could get struck by lightning up here.

I shimmy back down the tree and drop from a low branch. My face hits the ground and I get a mouth full of mud. I wipe my face with my sleeve.

'Bandit?' I ask, quickly checking that he's OK. He scurries up behind my neck.

Lightning forks through the sky with a thwack. The tree that was leaning bends and breaks in half. My heart leaps. I almost climbed that tree.

'Thank goodness we chose the other tree,' I whisper to Bandit.

The storm's close now. The moon is blocked by the clouds and it is pitch black under the trees. I have to find shelter further away from the storm. The sky cracks again. I turn and run.

Seb

Midway Geyser Basin, Yellowstone

4th July, 3 a.m.

♥ THE FOUR OF HEARTS ♥

It turns out the cliffs are further away than I thought. Anxiety is creeping through my chest again. I've been walking for what feels like hours. I can't have an anxiety attack now, I have to find Vivi and save Clay.

Just when I think I'm there I hear the flow of water and see a river blocking my path. It's just too wide to jump over and it's moving too swiftly to wade through — plus it looks deep. I can't risk getting wet, I could get hypothermia.

I search with the torch for a safe place to cross, but I can't see anywhere. Around me, branches are breaking off the trees in the wind and falling to the ground. If I can just make it across then I can shelter under the cliffs until the wind dies down.

One of the fallen branches is thick and long — almost like a small tree trunk — and I get an idea. I touch my foot to it and press down, testing its strength. I think it will hold my weight.

It's heavy, but I drag it across the ground to the river and manage to lift it on its end, then topple it over so it's balanced across the water.

I reach into my pocket for the familiar comfort of my deck of cards. I can't help but swiftly pick one.

The four of hearts again.

This isn't going to be easy.

I take a deep breath and place one foot on the

branch. Slowly, I inch along the branch, tight-roping, sticking my arms out to balance. Bark flakes off under my shoes.

It reminds me of the time in the game when we were trying to save the Amazon River from being polluted. We had to travel down it on a raft. I'd persuaded a group of loggers (Clay did their voices) to let us use their raft using my telepathic abilities. Once we were in the river, the current was bad, and Ava used her club super strength to keep us from capsizing. Then the polluted water splashed into the boat and Zac had to shield us from it using his diamond indestructability.

I wish I had a diamond shield from the rain and wind right now. I'm halfway across the river and my fingers hurt from the cold. I look down and see the water rushing underneath me and wobble. My chest tightens.

I can't have an attack now. I try the breathing exercise. It's not working. What was the next thing Christine suggested? I stare at my surroundings and try and think about five things that I can touch. The log. The water beneath it. My heart races. I'm feeling more scared. My surroundings are the very things giving me an anxiety attack.

Christine said some people like to say the alphabet backwards or list all the states of America. The only thing I can think to list is dinosaurs: Tyrannosaurus rex, Velociraptor, Diplodocus, Stegosaurus, Brachiosaurus, Allosaurus. My breaths slow. It's working. Triceratops. I focus on my breathing. In for one, two, three. Out for one, two, three.

Vivi's close by. She has to be. I slowly begin to creep across the log again until I reach the other side of the river. Shakily I stumble forward to the shelter of the cliffs.

Vivi

Midway Geyser Basin, Yellowstone

4th July, 3.50 a.m.

This can't be happening. I can't be lost in Yellowstone Park during a lightning storm. I feel the same sense of disbelief as when Dad told me about Grandma. *This can't be real.*

'Help!' I shout.

The storm is on top of me now. It starts raining big droplets. I run, stumbling over tree roots in the dark. The wind and rain sting my face.

'Seb!' I scream, again and again. The pounding rain drowns out my shouts.

I stop and huddle under a wide tree, letting the warmth from Bandit curled up inside my jacket comfort me. The branches of the tree block most of the droplets. I slide down against the trunk and pull my knees up to my chest and hug them. Why can't I find Seb? *What if the bear* . . . I don't want to finish the thought. I don't think I've ever been so scared in my life.

I remember how worried I was about Dad discovering the truth about the audition. Right now, I *wish* the stupid audition was my only problem. I'd confess everything in an instant if it meant getting out of here alive.

I pull the blanket from my backpack and wrap it around my shoulders and lean my head against the trunk. Around me the sky lights up in flashes of lightning. I can't believe Seb got me to agree to doing something so stupid.

What was I thinking?

The wind howls and I picture Grandma protecting me in every rustle of leaf. I remember the satsuma and orange trees that grew in her yard and how at Thanksgiving everyone would take bags of them home, except me and Dad who couldn't take them on the plane. We would eat as many as we possibly could before we left, and would leave with the scent of oranges on our hands. I let my eyes close, imagining being in her safe, warm, dry house.

I feel the earth shudder and I snap my eyes open. The ground is motionless around me. Did I dream it?

Seb

Midway Geyser Basin, Yellowstone

4th July, 4.50 a.m.

 THE ACE OF HEARTS

I remember from my school project that Yellowstone can have thousands of earthquakes a year but most of them aren't even felt by humans.

Well, I DEFINITELY JUST FELT AN EARTHQUAKE.

The whole ground rumbled and the cliff above me shook. I wonder what magnitude it was. I pull out a card, hoping for reassurance. It's an ace. My second critical fail of the night. Not a good omen.

I sigh. The storm's moving on and the rain's stopped and I want to start searching for Vivi again, but I'm worried there'll be another tremor. It must be a few hours since we saw the bear and I lost Vivi.

A bird flies overhead and it reminds me of my argument with Clay. I was right; a Pterodactyl is *not* a dinosaur. But it doesn't matter. I'd agree that it was a dinosaur, if I could just see Clay again and know that he was going to be OK. And who knows, maybe he's right about Pterodactyls. (He's not.)

I wish I could have told him that. I don't want our last words to have been an argument.

Twigs crack in the distance. Something big is moving through the forest. *Please, not another bear.* I clap my hands loudly, just in case, then risk calling out.

'VIVI? Is that you?'

No response. I shake my head. What an awful situation I've put us in. I shouldn't have insisted we go tonight.

I hear rustling again, but it sounds further away now. If it is Vivi, I'm losing her. I cross the river again, crawling across my log as quickly as possible and then break into a run.

'VIVI!' I shout, heading towards the sounds, clapping as I go. I hear the trickle of running water. Is it the river again? Have I gone in a circle? I look over my shoulder to check, and when I turn back, a shadow is looming above me.

I skid to a halt, shining the torch upwards to see what it is. I take a step back, and my centre of gravity shifts. I'm falling.

I put out my hands to regain my balance, reaching out behind me to try and break my fall — but the ground never comes.

Vivi

Midway Geyser Basin, Yellowstone

4th July, 4.55 a.m.

The storm has died down and the moon is back out. In the howl of the wind, I think I hear my name.

'Seb?' I shout.

I listen. Nothing, except the wind in the trees. Was it even him? Am I hearing things? Which direction did it come from?

I clutch Bandit in my arms and slowly walk in the direction I think it came from. Shining the torch across the ground in front of me, I move onwards through the darkness. My heart races.

'Grandma,' I whisper. 'If you are a ghost, right now would be a great time to use any powers you might have. I could do with some protection.'

The more I think about it, the more certain I am that I did hear my name. I clamber up a boulder slope and through a sparsely wooded plain. I reach the top of the hill.

'Come on, Seb!' I shout. 'Try again!'

It's the least he can do. True, I ran away from the bear but he's the one that got us into this mess. I stop and adjust my jacket, hot after climbing. I hear the gush of running water and shine the torch around the ground. A thin river runs over the side of the hill. I inch towards the edge. From the light of the moon I watch the water cascade down a narrow waterfall into a pool at the bottom. Then I see something that makes my knees feel weak.

There's someone struggling in the pool.

Seb.

I put Bandit into my pocket and scramble as fast as I can down the rocky side. It's wet and slippery. My feet search for footholds as I find rocks and tree roots to grab on to, slowly lowering myself down.

Below me, I can see Seb, thrashing in the water. The bank around the pool looks steep and slimy. How do I get him out? I remember the leaflet and how a person dissolved in one of these pools. Oh my God, what if Seb starts dissolving?

'Seb!' I scream. My feet touch solid ground. I shine the torch on Seb.

'Vivi,' he splutters. 'Is that you?'

He's alive. He's definitely alive. Not dissolving.

'Hang on,' I shout. 'I'm going to get you out, OK? Can you swim over to me?'

I see him splashing and swimming towards me.

I lie on my stomach and stretch my hand out. The water is freezing, colder than I ever could have imagined. Seb splashes closer. His icy cold hand clasps mine and I pull with all my might.

He grasps at the side of the bank and kicks his legs trying to find a foothold, but he keeps slipping back down. I heave until he can grab on to the edge of the bank with his other hand.

I wrap my arm around his waist and drag him up. We tumble onto the bank.

He splutters and coughs.

'I'm so glad you're here,' I say, hugging him tightly. 'I thought you'd been eaten by the bear.'

'I can't believe you found me!' he says, through chattering teeth.

'Are you in pain?' I ask.

'No, I'm cold. Really, really cold.' He grips my hand. 'We made it, Vivi,' he says.

'Where?' I ask.

'We made it to the rainbow pool.'

He's not making any sense. His speech is slurred. I touch his cheek. It's freezing.

'You have to get out of those wet clothes,' I tell him, trying not to sound as worried as I feel.

I'm wearing thermals underneath all of my layers and I quickly slip them off. They're stretchy and will fit him better than any of my normal clothes. I get re-dressed under the blanket. Then I hand him the blanket and a jumper from my backpack, along with my hat and gloves.

As he gets dressed, I look around at the landscape, hoping to see something that will help us. The sky is clear again and the full moon shines brightly. I see steam rising through the trees. The hydrothermal areas are warm. We have to get there. It's our only chance of not freezing to death.

'I'm dressed,' says Seb. 'I'm feeling a bit better.'

I take his wet clothes and shove them into his backpack. There's a soggy notebook inside. I squeeze it out as much as I can and move it to my own dry backpack. My hand rubs against the flask of hot chocolate and I grab it and hand it to him.

'This should help too,' I say.

He takes a sip and nods.

'Can you walk?' I ask, desperate to get him to warmth.

'I think so,' he replies, but he sounds unsure.

I clasp his trembling fingers in mine and lead him forwards, towards the plumes of steam.

'Do you still think we're at the rainbow pool?' I ask, after a few minutes. I've been too scared to ask until now. What if he still isn't making sense? What do I do then?

'No,' he shakes his head. His voice is sad and defeated. 'I got confused. We're lost. But at least we've found each other.'

In spite of his tone, relief floods through me. I squeeze his hand. 'I'm so glad you're alive!' I say, half-laughing, half-crying.

'Thanks to you. You basically saved my life back there,' he says.

I smile in the darkness. 'Well, you saved us from the bear.'

'So now we're even,' says Seb.

I nod. 'Even,' I repeat.

After twenty minutes we reach a huge simmering pool that stinks of rotten eggs. In one corner of it, water bubbles and erupts, constantly spraying droplets into the air. We huddle together next to it, warming up in the heat from the steam and each other. Seb opens his backpack and looks inside.

'Where's the handbook?' he asks, his voice tense.

'Oh, I put it in here,' I say reaching for my backpack.

'Thank you,' says Seb, sounding relieved. I pass it to him and he opens and fans the pages, trying to dry them.

After a few minutes he asks, 'Do you have my pack of cards too? They were in my pocket.'

I yank his wet trousers from the backpack and check his pocket. The cards are there, along with a chocolate bar.

Seb beams and takes the cards from me, carefully peeling them apart, laying each one out in front of us to dry.

I reach into my own pocket to cuddle Bandit, but he doesn't move as I touch him. I lift him out. He's as limp as a rag.

'Bandit,' I whisper. 'Are you OK?'

'What's wrong with him?' asks Seb.

'I don't know,' I reply, gently shaking him. He doesn't stir, not even a twitch.

Please wake up, Bandit.

Seb

Midway Geyser Basin, Yellowstone
4th July, 5.20 a.m.

♥ THE QUEEN OF HEARTS ♥

'Why won't he wake up?' asks Vivi. Tears stream down her face.

Bandit lies on his side across Vivi's lap. I stroke his tummy. He doesn't flinch.

Vivi picks him up and examines him. 'I don't see any injuries,' she says.

Bandit is floppy in her hands.

'Please wake up,' Vivi says. 'Please.'

My heart aches for her. I hope something didn't happen to Bandit while she was saving me from the pool.

When I'd slipped, I'd thought for sure that I was about to be dissolved in a hot acidic volcanic pool. But it was just one of the watering holes that's fed from the river.

I panicked when I hit the water. Once I realised I couldn't get out of the slippery bank, I started calculating how long I could survive in the icy water before going unconscious. I'd almost given up when Vivi came.

I wish I could help her now like she helped me.

She's cradling Bandit in her arms. I touch his tiny chest, searching for a heartbeat.

'He's warm,' I say and then under my fingertip I feel the tiny flutter of a heartbeat. It's much faster than mine. 'Here,' I say and guide Vivi's hand to feel it too. 'He's alive.'

Vivi sobs and cuddles him.

Suddenly, Bandit opens his mouth widely and yawns. He sleepily opens his eyes and looks at us both.

'Oh, Bandit!' says Vivi. 'You scared me!'

I let out a huge breath, relief washing over me. 'What was wrong with him?' I ask.

Vivi shakes her head. 'I have no idea. Maybe he was cold or got really scared and was playing dead. Do ferrets do that?'

I shrug. 'I don't know.'

Vivi reaches out and takes my hand and together we watch Bandit scamper between us as we warm up by the steaming pool.

♠ ♣ ♥ ♦

After a while, Vivi asks, 'Should we keep going?'

I nod. I feel much stronger now. But as I stand, a wave of dizziness hits me. I sit back down.

'Maybe in a few minutes,' I say.

We lean against each other and it starts drizzling.

'I don't know what I would have done if I'd lost Grandma *and* Bandit,' says Vivi, stroking the ferret.

'I think I met your grandma,' I say. Now seems like the right time to tell Vivi. 'In the gas station.'

She stares at me, eyes wide.

'How do you know it was her? What did she say? Did she seem happy? What was she doing?'

I tell her how she'd wanted a cold lemonade from the back of the fridge, how I realised it was her later on because of the pink scarf.

'I wish there was more that I could tell you,' I say. 'She called me "darling".'

Vivi wraps her arms around her body, gazing out over the bubbling pool and sighs. 'That sounds like Grandma. I'm glad she got to meet you.'

Bandit scurries up onto my arm and nuzzles into my neck.

Vivi stares up at the stars. There are more stars visible here than I've ever seen anywhere before. Whole galaxies.

'Grandma always said we were made of stardust,' says Vivi.

'It's true,' I reply.

Vivi laughs. 'Really? I thought it was one of her folktales.'

'It's pretty much true; most of the elements of our bodies were formed in stars over the course of billions of years.'

The playing cards have dried out a bit.

'Want to learn how to play Calamity Stoppers?' I ask.

She nods and I teach her by moonlight. Her first card is the queen of hearts. She's brilliant at it. Clay would be impressed.

Vivi

Midway Geyser Basin, Yellowstone

4th July, 5.35 a.m.

By the time Seb's taught me the game it's getting light and birdsong fills the air. It's been fun. And it took my mind off everything for a while and that was nice.

Knowing that Seb was one of the last people to see Grandma makes me want to be near him, like it'll get me closer to her too.

'What were you doing on that day?' asks Seb. 'The day of the shooting?'

I gaze out at the brightening horizon. 'Failing my audition.'

'Wait.' Seb sits up. 'I thought you aced that audition. You got the part!'

'I lied,' I say, and it feels good to say it out loud. 'I forgot all my lines. It was a disaster.' I cringe remembering it.

'I bet your grandma failed plenty of auditions too,' says Seb.

'Maybe. She probably didn't lie about it though,' I reply.

'Don't be too hard on yourself about what you can't change,' says Seb. 'Just do what you can to make it right.'

I agree with him. And a part of me can't wait to tell Dad and even Mum. I just want to get it over with. I'm done being scared.

Seb stands on tip-toes, looking around us. Now that it's light I can see we're in a valley with hills all around us.

'Shall we try and find the rainbow pool now?'
I ask, standing next to him.

He turns and grins at me. 'Onwards!' he says
and gestures forwards.

'If we get to the top of that hill over there we
might be able to see it,' I say, pointing at the
tallest hill around us.

'It's a plan,' says Seb.

Bandit nuzzles into my neck.

I grasp Seb's hand and, avoiding the steam
rising off the pools and the vents pluming from
the earth, we venture out into the wilderness.

Seb

Midway Geyser Basin, Yellowstone

4th July, 5.35 a.m.

♥ THE SEVEN OF HEARTS ♥

I'm still feeling a bit cold and shivery but the heat from Vivi's hand warms me. I'm pretty sure she saved my life. And now we've got to save Clay's. A dawn chorus of twitters and birdsong fills the air.

The light shifts. It's finally morning. I get out my deck of cards to examine the water damage. The seven of hearts is on top. Its corners are curled but there's no damage to the face of it. I flick through the rest of the pack.

Suddenly, the ground rumbles and shakes underneath me, more violently than the time before. I look to Vivi. She's frozen. Bandit dives back into her pocket. Then the movement stops.

'Er, what was that?' says Vivi.

'I think it was a geyser going off,' I say hopefully.

'This volcano isn't about to erupt is it?' asks Vivi.

'I don't *think* so,' I say. 'It hasn't erupted for over six hundred thousand years.'

'Oh my God,' says Vivi, 'That means it's probably due for an eruption! After surviving the bear and the lightning, I'm going to be killed by molten hot lava! You've got to be kidding me.' She's pacing back and forth, raising her hands in the air. 'Or will the gases kill us first? Am I breathing them in now?'

'Listen to me,' I say. 'It's not erupting. It probably won't erupt for another hundred thousand years and there are so many scientists monitoring it, we'd know if . . .'

But Vivi's not listening.

'Oh God, oh God, oh God,' she says. 'They'll only be able to identity me by my teeth, everything else will be gone. Or will my teeth dissolve too?'

'You're going to be fine,' I say.

'And I didn't get a chance to tell Dad the truth about the audition. This is terrible. I won't have a chance to explain.'

'IT'S NOT ERUPTING!' I say loudly.

'Oh,' Vivi says. 'Are you sure?'

'I'm sure.'

'Then what on earth was that?'

I think I know, but I don't want to freak her out even more. 'It might have been a teeny tiny earthquake.'

'An *earthquake*?'

'Don't freak out. They happen all the time because there's magma beneath us. And movement. Or something like that. If I'm being totally honest, I don't remember exactly why there's so many earthquakes.'

'This is supposed to be helping?' Vivi asks, clearly not impressed.

So I say the only thing I can think of that

might help. 'What do you call a dinosaur's fart?'
I ask.

'Now's not the time for jokes, Seb,' she says.

I continue anyway. 'A blast from the past.'

And she starts laughing.

Vivi

Midway Geyser Basin, Yellowstone

4th July, 6 a.m.

Seb's silly joke sets me off laughing. After everything we've been through, it doesn't feel like there's anything else to do.

I'm so tired. I can't stop laughing. The joke's not even funny.

We continue walking and pass a geyser. Steam billows off the surface, the rising sun turning it orange. It's eerie, how I'd imagine Mars to look. Beyond the geyser is an opening in the forest that stretches all the way to the bottom of the steep hill we want to climb up. We head towards the clearing. It's flat and marshy.

A herd of bison are grazing in the clearing, birds on their backs.

'Look!' Seb says. 'There's a boardwalk the other side of them that must lead to the hill. That's where we need to go!'

I give him a sceptical look. After the charging bear, I don't want to get close to any more wild animals.

'We'll be OK if we stay twenty-five yards away from them,' says Seb.

'Dad says that bison are the most dangerous animals in the park. The leaflet said that the bulls can be unpredictable,' I say. 'If they raise their tails, it's a sign they might charge.'

'We can go around them,' he says.

The air is quiet. There are no car engines or

people chattering, only birds singing and the breathing of the bison.

We edge around the clearing, trying to be quiet and not startle the bison, but there are lots of twigs and dry leaves underfoot. Several lift their heads and look towards the trees in our direction. One bison begins to grunt, then another joins in. I notice the younger ones are gathering in the middle of the group.

'What are they doing?' I ask. 'Are we too close?'

'Let's stop for a minute,' says Seb.

We kneel and lie on our stomachs, watching from a distance.

'I think they might be protecting their young,' I say, realising the biggest bison are all in an outer circle, surrounding the young ones. 'Let's back away.'

'But we're too small to be a threat to them,' says Seb.

I shake my head. 'They keep looking over to the right. There must be a different predator nearby.'

In my mind, I list the animals I saw on the leaflet I was given at the park's entrance: mountain lions, coyotes, wolves, bears.

None of them sound good.

'Let's get out of here,' I say.

We continue around the clearing in the opposite direction to the potential bison predator. The landscape in front of us is flat and sparse and surrounded by hills. Pockets of steam rise from the ground.

In the quiet I notice a new sound. I think it's a geyser erupting in the distance at first, but then I realise the noise is coming from someplace much closer. It's not a geyser at all; it's the sound of water, boiling.

Seb

Midway Geyser Basin, Yellowstone

4th July, 6.30 a.m.

♥ THE FIVE of HEARTS ♥

I'm anxious to get to the pool and then back to the camp soon so that I can sort out my story before Mom wakes up. I haven't decided what I'll tell her. Maybe that I encountered a bear outside the toilets? I instinctively reach for my cards and pull one to see the likelihood of that plan working. The five of hearts. Sounds about right. I doubt she'd believe the bear story.

We're almost at the boardwalk I saw on the other side of the bison. The ground around it is muddy.

'Seb,' calls Vivi from behind me. 'Stop for a minute. Come back here.'

Her voice is quiet, but there's something in her tone that makes me stop immediately. Before I have time to look around, the earth beneath my foot cracks and my shoe sinks through the ground. A searing pain shoots up my leg.

I yank my foot straight out again.

I glance down, feeling strangely calm. The mud below my foot is bubbling. It's not red. It's water. If it was lava I guess my whole foot would have melted off.

The water touched my ankle. That's the bit that hurts the most. I examine it. My skin's burning. Badly. It's deep and gross and oozing.

'Oh my God, Seb! Are you OK?' Vivi calls, frozen to the spot.

'Don't come any nearer,' I say.

I realise how stupid we've been. There was a boardwalk leading to the geyser because this whole area is bubbling mud. It's volcanic. I think about the person who dissolved in the pool. I wonder if that's what will happen to my foot?

'Don't move,' I say to Vivi. I look around me at the mud. Somehow, we've walked far into the bubbling mudpots without sinking. Further ahead there's no crust at all and I can see the wet mud erupting and moving. I wonder if we could go back the way we came? But there's no way to step in exactly the same places. And I'm not sure if the crust will hold us a second time, even if we could remember our exact path back.

I try and weigh up the risks in my head. Vivi is staring in horror at the ground around her. There's a small plop as the mud next to her explodes and she gives a shriek.

My foot throbs in agony. I want to plunge myself into an ice-cold bath but everything around here is hot. Burning pain shoots through my skin and leg.

I have to know if it's dissolving my skin and bones. The material of my pants is sticking to my ankle and I rip it off, gritting my teeth but not able to stop a yell from coming out. I force myself to look at it again. It's still gross but the burn hasn't changed much. I take that as a good sign.

At least I'm still standing. Whatever happens, I can't let myself fall into the volcano.

Vivi

Midway Geyser Basin, Yellowstone
4th July, 6.35 a.m.

Ahead of me, Seb's trying to balance on his uninjured leg, but he's wobbling. I can't see how badly injured he is.

'Keep talking to me,' I say, although I'm hardly listening to what he's saying. I'm trying to process our surroundings and scan for a way out of here. Would anyone ever find us if we fell into the bubbling mudpots? Bandit has decided to pretend it's all not happening and has fallen asleep in my pocket.

'What do I do?' I whisper to him.

I wish Dad was here. I wish we had never tried to find the rainbow pool by ourselves. Why did I agree to go? Why didn't I insist we turn around after we were nearly eaten by a bear? Or after we were almost electrocuted in a storm? Or after Seb nearly drowned in a waterfall?

I try to stay still but as soon as I focus on it, not moving becomes harder. I pretend I'm in a film, anything to make this not real. It actually helps a bit until I imagine us being rescued and I realise that in real life there's no one coming to save us. No one even knows we're here.

'Help!' I shout. 'Anyone out there? Help!' My cries are lost in the trees.

'My other leg's starting to cramp,' says Seb. 'I don't know how much longer I can stay here.'

'I'll try and come to you,' I say, although I've no idea how to make that a reality.

I hear a rustling behind me.

I turn. Goosebumps prickle up and down my arm.

Behind me are three wolves and a wolf pup.

They watch us. The one at the front is obviously the leader of the pack, the alpha. She has dark, almost black fur, yellowy-orange eyes and pointed ears. A mane of fur runs down the back of her neck. She stands taller than the others, with stiff legs and her tail high.

The other two are grey with white on their faces and feet. They look almost like gigantic huskies. Our neighbour has a pet husky, Snowball, who loves licking my ears. But these are wild creatures and they're looking straight at me.

I'm filled with the same fear as when we faced the bear. Only this time there's nowhere to run to.

Seb hasn't noticed the wolves yet. I don't want him to see them and lose his balance.

'Seb,' I whisper. My voice sticks in the back of my throat. I don't dare speak any louder.

The pup's forelegs are splayed wide. It wags its tail, almost like it's inviting me to play. I notice the pup is holding its front paw up, as if hurt.

The wolves walk closer towards me, with the alpha leading. My breath is loud no matter how hard I try to quieten it.

My stomach turns. 'Please,' I whisper. 'I won't hurt you.' I stay, frozen to the spot.

Then they pass right by me and walk up to Seb. I gasp, fear rising in my chest. Can they sense he's injured, weak? But just before they reach him, they turn away, towards the woods.

He's looking the other way and hasn't even noticed them. They walk in a line, one by one, each stepping in the alpha's paw prints. The alpha stops and looks back at me with her orange eyes. And, that's when I realise; they're avoiding the mudpots. They know where to step.

'Seb?' I say, louder this time.

He turns and spots the wolves for the first time. I see his eyes widen in panic. 'It's OK,' I say. 'They're not going to hurt us. I know how to get out of here. We can follow the wolves.'

He shakes his head.

'Listen to me,' I say. 'Do you see their paw prints in the mud?'

'I see them,' he says.

'Step into the one next to you,' I instruct. He gently puts his injured foot down into the one closest to him.

It holds and I let out a sigh of relief. I walk in the paw prints towards him. The mud creaks and bubbles under my feet but it doesn't crack. I make it to Seb, and he leans on me.

'It's my ankle that's the worst,' he says. 'My walking boots saved my feet I think.'

The alpha wolf has been watching us. She licks her pup. It's grey with streaks of black on it. They walk ahead and, slowly, at a distance, we follow them, stepping carefully in their paw prints, Seb still using my shoulder for support. It's as if the wolves are leading us out of the dangerous mud.

They're saving our lives.

They reach the boardwalk and jump up it and then immediately back down onto the other side. I continue to lead Seb, gingerly following the wolves' tracks. With each new step, I catch my breath, hoping the ground will hold until we reach the boardwalk.

We climb up onto the muddy planks, and I let out a huge breath. Though she's already halfway to the trees, the alpha stops and looks back at me. I notice she has flecks of grey around her face. 'Thank you,' I whisper, as I watch them disappear into the trees.

Wolf howls fill the air. My skins prickles. They're howling together in a chorus of different tones. The pack finishes as one but the high-pitched wolf pup howl continues for a second longer, maybe not knowing when to stop.

I smile.

'They're saying goodbye,' Seb says.

'Should we say goodbye back?' I ask.

He nods.

I lift my head and look up at the wispy clouds, white against the deep-blue sky. A raven flies above us and settles on a branch, watching us.

I close my eyes and howl. I feel my feet grounded in the earth and think of Grandma.

Seb

Midway Geyser Basin, Yellowstone

4th July, 6.45 a.m.

♥ THE JACK OF HEARTS ♥

Clay was always saying that wolves came from a time before humans, and that they were a symbol of the freedom of the wild. Seeing them reminds me of him. It's as if he's here, helping me make it to the rainbow pool.

'Was that even real?' I ask, staring at Vivi. 'Or did I imagine those wolves?'

'They were real,' she says. She's looking at me in a way that usually only Clay looks at me and I know that we've shared something secret, something special. I'll remember it for the rest of my life.

In the game, the wolves are what we'd call a good omen in a campaign. I think about reaching the rainbow pool and instinctively reach for a card. The jack of hearts.

I feel a flutter of hope that, after all of this, we're really going to make it. The pain in my ankle is subsiding; maybe my body is in shock. I remember when I broke my arm snowboarding. After the initial pain it didn't hurt that much, but later it was awful.

I have to get to the rainbow pool before the shock wears off.

The sun is still low in the sky and there's no heat from it yet. I shiver.

'I think we've had all the luck we can possibly have,' Vivi says. 'We've got to get out of here before something else happens.'

'OK,' I say, thinking that there's no way I'm giving up now. If I can find the pool, I'm going. No one can stop me. I've come this far. I start to lead Vivi up the hill, hoping that I can see the rainbow pool from the top.

'Oh my God, I can't go any further,' says Vivi, dragging her feet. 'I just can't. Let's lie down here and wait for someone to find us.'

'Just a bit further,' I urge. I point to the top of the hill. 'We'll be more likely to be seen on a high point.'

But I can tell Vivi knows why I really want to go.

'We're not going to find it, Seb. We've been looking *all* night. Bandit's ready to go home,' Vivi says.

I peek at him, curled up and fast asleep in her arms.

'He seems fine,' I say. 'Look, as soon as we find our parents that will be it. I won't get a chance to make the wish again. They'll take us home straight away.'

'But I'm so tired and we've almost died out here, more than once! Clay wouldn't want that, would he?'

For a split second I wonder if she's right about that. But then I remember how much the wish will mean to him.

'Clay's having his operation this morning,' I

reply. 'He needs the wish now more than ever. I'd carry you if I could.'

Vivi laughs. 'I'd like to see you try. Even if you weren't burnt, I'm way taller than you. Besides I don't need carrying. I'll keep going.'

We continue trudging up the side of the slope.

'Those bison were protecting their young from the wolves,' I say, trying to distract Vivi from how tired she is. 'I can't wait to tell Mom. If I ever see her again. After I told her about the elephants she found a documentary about it. I bet there are some good documentaries about bison.'

We pass an erupting geyser, spraying water high into the air. It rests for a minute then begins erupting again. Halfway up the lightly wooded hillside, there's a path. I stumble. The pain in my leg rushes back and I yelp.

'Here, let me help you,' says Vivi.

I lean on her and try to hobble but waves of heat and pain shoot through my leg and my foot gives way.

'I'll give you a piggyback,' says Vivi.

I wince as I get on. My foot feels as if it's about to fall off. We come up onto a ridge and I gaze out over it. We're overlooking a wide, flat valley. The land is bare and scarred white. But there, in the centre of the bleakness, right below us, is the biggest pool I've ever seen. It looks bigger than a football field. Around the outside is a band of red, which turns to bright orange, then yellow and green. In the centre of the ring of colours is a circle of bright blue. My heart skips.

It's Clay's rainbow pool. I just know it.

I remember learning how the multicoloured layers get their hues from different species of heat-loving bacteria living in the water around the spring. The bacteria change colours as the temperature changes. And the centre is deep blue because water scatters the blue wavelengths of light more than others, reflecting blues back to our eyes.

I take a deep breath and slide off Vivi's back. I've made it to the Grand Prismatic Spring. It looks just like Clay's drawings. His map could have had more detail, but the drawing was right.

Pressure lifts from my chest as relief floods over me. I made it. Now we just have to make the wish.

Vivi

Midway Geyser Basin, Yellowstone

4th July, 7.30 a.m.

I can tell from the smile on Seb's face that we've made it. The rainbow pool below us bubbles and steams. Clouds of mist rise from it. The outer rust-coloured ring of the pool runs and flows in streams onto the land around it. The pool reminds me of an eye, with the deep, bright-blue centre being the pupil and the coloured rings and wiggly lines from the flow being the iris.

Then I notice the best thing. Beyond the pool is a road!

'Is this it?' I ask. 'Is this really it?'

Seb's eyes are wide and excited even though he is pale. 'Yeah. We did it.'

I squeal and accidently wake Bandit up, who climbs onto my head, takes one look at the bubbling pool and disappears quickly down my sleeve.

'Are you going to make your wish?' I ask.

'We have to do that together, remember,' he says. 'Those are Clay's rules.'

'How do we do it?' I ask.

There's a faint sheen of sweat on Seb's skin. I want to get him help as soon as possible.

Seb pulls the handbook from his backpack and clutches it to his chest. 'At least two people must make the wish together,' he says. 'And they have to agree on what the wish will be.'

'And then what?' I say.

'We've completed the campaign. We just have to get back and claim our reward.'

'What's the reward?' I ask.

'My friend Clay getting better.'

For a split second, I think about wishing that I *did* get the part of Alice, but I stop myself. Telling the truth about what happened in the audition doesn't feel as scary any more. Besides, there will be other auditions, other parts. As Grandma would say, it wasn't meant to be. And Seb said that we have to make the same wish for it to work anyway.

'Are you ready?' I ask.

Seb nods and holds out his hand. I take it. 'One, two . . .'

Before we get to three, his hand yanks out of mine and he slumps to the ground. I drop to my knees next to him.

'Seb?' I say.

There's no response. I can see his chest moving, so I know he's breathing, but he's not waking up. *What do I do?*

I think back to when I couldn't wake Bandit up. What did I do then? It's easier to focus when I think of Bandit and not Seb.

'I checked you for injuries,' I whisper to Bandit.

I pull back the material of the thermals Seb's wearing by his foot. 'Oh no,' I whisper.

Underneath, his skin is swollen and leathery. Giant red blisters ooze. What if there was poison in that boiling mud?

'Seb,' I say, gently shaking him.

He needs to wake up. He has to.

I reach for the flask of hot chocolate. There's a little left. I prop him up and raise it to his lips.

I see his eyes flutter and a moment later he comes round.

'How are you feeling?' I ask.

'I've felt better,' he says, managing a weak smile.

In the side part of the backpack there's another chocolate bar and a packet of biscuits. The hot chocolate woke him up and all I can think to do is feed them to him.

'Seb, that burn . . .' I say. 'It doesn't look good.' *That's an understatement*, I think to myself. 'We need to get help.'

'The wish,' he says. 'Let's do the wish first.' He crawls to the edge of the overhang, and lies on his stomach looking out over the pool.

I know that everything he's been through has been for this wish, so I join him. And the truth is, I understand. If I could make a wish to see Grandma again, just once, I'd do anything to make it happen.

'One, two, three . . .' says Seb.

'I wish for Clay to get better,' we both say, slowly so that we can say it at the same time, and the words float out to join the steam rising from the spring, to be carried into the sky.

'Did it work?' Seb asks quietly. 'What does the handbook say?'

I take the handbook from him, open it to the very last page and read. 'After you've made the wish, the rainbow pool starts to change colour, from azure blue to lava red before turning to a glowing yellow. The pool bubbles and erupts, shooting towers of water into the air with loud roars and whooshes. Finally, it settles back to its rainbow state. And that's when you know the wish has been granted.'

Below us thick steam blows over the top of the surface, hiding the pool beneath it. That's when I see a rainbow in the steam, right in front of us.

'A double rainbow,' Seb murmurs, before dropping his head down.

'I think it worked, Seb,' I whisper.

'I think so too,' he says.

I scan the horizon, trying to figure out a way to get to the road. There should be more people around by now, surely. The sun has risen. There were plenty of people at Old Faithful yesterday.

'I think it's that way,' I say, pointing back down the hill and to the right.

'I can't walk any further,' says Seb, and I can hear the pain in his voice.

'Then we'll just lie here and I'll stay with you,' I say, though I'm worried about how long it will take for help to arrive. No one knows where we are. And Seb needs a hospital now.

He rolls over and we lie back against the ridge overlooking the spring. The steam rises into the sky. I feed Bandit ferret food from my palm.

'Here,' I say, passing him the ferret. 'Snuggle Bandit. He'll make you feel better.'

Seb smiles but his face is strained. His skin is cold to touch and his foot oozes. I'm more scared than I was when I ran from the bear, or when I saw the wolves or felt the earthquake, because I know that Seb could die out here. I close my eyes and hope with all my might that he can hold on until help comes.

Seb

Midway Geyser Basin, Yellowstone

4th July, 7.40 a.m.

♥ THE ACE OF HEARTS ♥

I lean my head back against the slope. The pain has got so much worse since we made it to the rainbow pool. Heat radiates up my whole leg.

I open and close my fist, wanting the familiar comfort of drawing a card from my deck but I don't even have the energy to reach into my pocket.

'They'll find us soon. There can't be that big of an area to search,' says Vivi.

'Actually, Yellowstone's about three and a half thousand square miles big.'

Vivi groans. 'You've got to be kidding me,' she says. 'At least I can see the road. The park's bound to open any second. I'll wave someone down.'

'They know the general area we're in, I guess,' I add hopefully. 'That will narrow it down a bit.'

I stare up at the blue sky. A raven flies overhead.

'Does it ever get easier?' Vivi asks quietly. 'After someone dies, I mean?'

I know she's talking about my dad. I think for a second. Her nose is red from the cold and her eyes shine.

'No,' I reply. 'It's just different. You get used to it eventually. It's a whole new reality. You learn to live with it.'

The sun has finally risen fully and I try to focus on the warmth of it on my face but the pain in my leg is becoming unbearable. My body tenses. I try and breathe deeply but I can't seem to catch my breath.

'We should have wished to go back in time,' says Vivi wistfully.

But the wish we did make is the one thing keeping me going right now. We did it in time for Clay's operation. I imagine us being together soon, sitting around a table, playing Calamity Stoppers, Vivi looking annoyed that she pulled an ace.

Vivi

Midway Geyser Basin, Yellowstone

4th July, 8.00 a.m.

I've felt Grandma with me in every part of this trip, as if she's been saying goodbye. I feel her next to me now.

'Grandma,' I whisper. 'If you're here with me, please help. Help me save Seb.'

His eyes are closed.

Why aren't there any other people round?

Then, far in the distance, I hear the thrum of an engine and see a car. It's a four-by-four driving through the park.

I stand on the top of the ridge and wave my arms up and down and scream at the top of my voice.

'Help!' I shout. 'Help!' Can they even see us? We must look like two tiny specks on top of a hill, overlooking the spring.

I have to get down to them. Seb's pale and hardly moving. His forehead is clammy.

I kneel next to him. 'I'm going to get help and I'll be right back. Just hang on.'

'Be quick,' he says.

'I will,' I reply. 'Here, keep Bandit with you for company.' I gently move Bandit onto Seb's chest, under the blanket draped round his shoulders, and slip Bandit's lead over Seb's wrist. Bandit curls up with his nose sticking out of the opening.

'Keep each other safe,' I whisper, then I dash down the slope, slipping on stones and catching myself. In the light of day, it's much easier to see where we are. I spot a dirt path leading in the direction of the road to the left. I'm out of breath but still scream as I run. 'We're here! We're here!'

I leap over a fallen branch. The path comes out in a car park. After being in the wilderness all night I can't believe we were this close to a car park. It was hidden by the trees and the curve of the hill. The car turns in a circle and begins to drive back the other way.

A stitch burns through my side. 'Please see me,' I yell. 'Please.' It's nearly at the exit.

I pick up a stone and hurl it as far as I possibly can. It pings off the back window. The car slows. I allow myself to stop and bend over. I've used up all the energy I had left.

The car stops and the door opens.

I cover my mouth with my hand and let out a sob of relief. Two park rangers run up to me, kneeling beside me. The man and woman wear matching uniforms with green jackets and hats.

'Are you hurt?' asks the woman. She's young and her hair is in two plaits.

I point to the ridge behind me. 'I'm OK. But my friend Seb is hurt. Really badly.'

The man telephones in for an air ambulance and a ground ambulance, stroking his big beard worriedly as he speaks.

They have a stretcher in the back of their car which they take out and carry. I lead them up the hill in a blur.

'We've been trying to find you for hours but an earthquake this morning caused some rocks to fall onto the main road so we couldn't drive up here. The park's been closed because it was such a big earthquake. You must have felt it.'

I nod. Just our luck there was a big earthquake the *one* night we decide to do something risky and venture out. We've almost reached Seb.

He's made it down the slope a bit. He's clutching his knee to his chest and groaning.

As we reach him, I hear the whirr of the helicopter landing in the car park.

Seb

Midway Geyser Basin, Yellowstone

4th July, 8.15 a.m.

 THE SIX OF HEARTS

I'm being lifted up on a stretcher. I stare up at the bright-blue sky. Six small fluffy clouds are clustered together. A six. Could be better, but could be worse. Then I close my eyes. I feel the warmth of Vivi's hand in mine. She chatters the whole way to the helicopter next to me.

I've never been in a helicopter before. It's loud. I try to sit up and see it.

'No,' says the paramedic. 'You need to stay lying down. Try and think calm thoughts. Why don't you think about your family?'

Think of my family? Isn't that something people say in someone's last moments? Do they think I'm GOING TO DIE?

My pulse quickens. Whatever happens, getting to the rainbow pool was worth it. I saved Clay. I know I did.

Vivi

Midway Geyser Basin, Yellowstone

4th July, 8.15 a.m.

There's no room for me in the helicopter. I squeeze Seb's hand goodbye and tell him that I'll see him soon.

The rangers take me and Bandit in the car, ushering me into the back seat.

'He'll be OK, right?' I ask.

'They're very good at treating burns at the hospital, I'm sure he'll be just fine,' the woman replies, turning around to face me from the passenger seat.

I think about how bad Seb's burn looked and try and believe her.

The man, who is driving, shakes his head. 'You were very fortunate it wasn't worse.' His voice is deep and gravelly.

I remember the wolves and the way the leader, the alpha, looked at me and licked her limping pup. They helped us and led us to safety. Maybe I could help her too.

'We saw a pack of wolves out there. The pup was limping. It might need help.'

'What did they look like?' she asks.

'The leader was black and then there were two that were grey.'

She shakes her head. 'I don't know which wolf pack you're talking about, but we'll have a look. You're lucky to have seen wolves.'

'I know,' I say and I whisper a silent 'thank you' to the wolves.

The rangers drive me to a big wooden lodge. Through the window I spot a group of people inside, two with cameras. After the quietness of the night, it feels busy and overwhelming.

'Your dad alerted us that you were missing around five this morning and we gathered a search party. But then the earthquake hit and we had to assess the extent of the damage before we let everyone look for you,' the man says.

'Are those reporters?' I ask, staring at the big cameras around their necks.

'Yeah, they came for news about the earthquake but they stayed when they heard that you two were missing,' explains the woman.

'They're here!' someone shouts as the woman ranger steps out of the car and opens the door for me. I see Dad pushing through the crowd and then he's grabbing me. He smells of wood smoke.

'Don't squash Bandit,' I say, almost crying. Bandit pops out of my jumper and settles in my hood.

'Please never run away again,' he says, squeezing me tightly.

'I didn't run away,' I say. 'We got lost. Wait, where's Seb's mum?'

'She's gone to the hospital already. I said we'd meet her there.'

Dad looks me up and down.

'Are you hurt? Do you need to go to the hospital too?'

I shake my head.

'What on earth were you thinking?' he says. 'You could have fallen in a ditch or been eaten by a mountain lion or goodness knows what else.'

'I'm sorry for worrying everyone,' I say, looking down. 'I never meant for you to even know I'd gone.'

'How long were they lost in the park?' interrupts a reporter, a clean-shaven man with spiky hair.

'Can this wait?' asks Dad, snapping at him.

Now's probably not the best time to tell him about the bear.

Then Dad hugs me fiercely again, dusting the dirt from my hair with trembling fingers. 'I'm just so happy to have you back.'

I go inside the lodge and I shower while Dad holds Bandit. Under the water, I squeeze my eyes open and shut. Our night in the park doesn't feel real.

Seb

Hospital, Wyoming
7th July, 11 a.m.

 THE NINE OF HEARTS

Everyone thought that we'd run away. I've had to tell the story of the rainbow pool seven times now. I keep trying to tell them that we always meant to come back before anyone noticed.

I've been in the hospital for three days. They had to operate on my skin and they've been keeping it clean for me and changing the dressing every day. It's actually pretty cool. They took some skin from my thigh and put it over the burnt skin on my foot.

Today's a big day. I'm being moved to a new hospital, back in Denver, the same one that Clay's in.

I keep waiting to be suddenly healed like in our game, but this is real life and I have to remember that some wounds heal slowly, like getting over the anxiety attacks.

Vivi's coming to say goodbye before she goes back to England. She's been visiting several times a day.

'How's Clay?' she asks, when she arrives.

'Still the same,' I say. The operation was a success but Mom says he's still in a 'critical condition'.

'Maybe the wish takes a little while to work?' she says.

'Yeah. At least the bullet is out of him,' I reply.

But it's hard not to feel disappointed. He was supposed to be better by now. 'I wish you didn't have to leave,' I say. My chest twinges with sadness that it's over.

'Come and visit me some day,' says Vivi. 'Did you bring Bandit with you?' I whisper. I want to say goodbye even though I know he's not supposed to be in here.

She looks around, checking there aren't any nurses or doctors nearby, before pulling a sleeping Bandit from her shoulder bag.

Bandit sees me and scampers across the bed, jumping and twisting in the air with excitement. He makes a little noise that sounds like 'dook, dook' before colliding into me.

Vivi and I both laugh.

I gently scoop him and hold him up to my cheek, which he nuzzles.

'He's going to miss you,' Vivi says.

'It won't be too long before we see each other again, right?' I ask.

'Definitely,' she says, tucking her hair behind her ear.

'You know, I think you saved my life out there *twice*. Thanks,' I say.

'No biggie,' Vivi says, jokingly. 'I do stuff like that *all* the time back at home.'

I laugh.

'Thanks for teaching me the game,' she says.

'You should keep a card,' I say, handing her the top of my deck. A nine of hearts. 'For luck.'

Vivi takes it and places it in her pocket. Then she hugs me gently. 'Next time we can play the game with Clay,' she says.

I smile. That sounds like the best thing in the world.

Vivi

Jackson Hole, Wyoming

7th July, 11 a.m.

Dad's hired a car to get us back to the Cadillac. We transfer our belongings from Seb's mum's car. She helps us pack.

'I'll have to flat-pack Bandit's cage to get it to fit,' he says.

'Oh that's fine, he's made a new home in my hood,' I say.

Dad empties the cage. 'Is this yours?' he asks, holding out a dangly earring.

'Grandma's earring!' I reply, taking it.

'Wait, there's something else,' says Dad. He pulls out a chain. On it hangs Seb's mum's ring.

Charlie beams and throws her arms around him. 'You found it!'

'Bandit took it?' I ask.

'Cheeky ferret,' says Dad. 'He's certainly living up to his name.'

Seb's mum turns to me. 'I'm so sorry, Vivi. I owe you an apology. Of course you wouldn't have touched my necklace.'

I smile. 'I'm just happy that you found it.'

Dad's quiet on the drive home and I can tell he's sad. He keeps sighing loudly. Bandit's curled up on my lap. I've spent the last three hours working up to telling him the truth about everything.

When we're almost back at the town where we left Cormac the Cadillac, he asks, 'Are you excited to get home and get stuck in to the part of Alice?' and I know it's time.

'Dad?' I say. 'I have something to tell you.'

'What is it, sweetie?' he asks.

'I didn't get the part of Alice.'

'You didn't make it through?' he asks, confused.

I shake my head. 'I didn't even finish the audition.'

'That's OK, bean. Why did you feel you had to lie about it?'

'I don't know. It just . . . happened. Grandma had died and everyone's always going on about how talented I am and I guess I didn't want to disappoint everyone. I worried you'd all think less of me. And — and if I'm not like Grandma . . . then she's really gone.'

He pulls the car over and looks at me. 'Sweetie, I will never think less of you.' He cups my face in his hands. 'OK?'

I nod and try to swallow the lump in my throat.

'And, wait for it . . .' He grabs my hands and studies them. 'Yes, I'm sorry to announce that you have the stubby Berry thumb. I have it, Grandma had it and you have too.'

'Get off,' I say, laughing and pulling my hand away.

He laughs too, but then looks at me seriously and I know he wants to say something important. 'Vivi, you're like Grandma in many more ways than your love of acting. You're kind and funny and incredibly strong-willed.'

I nod and even give him a small smile as the weight of it all lifts. I was feeling so much shame about my lie. Now that I've said it out loud, the feeling can't grow in the darkness any more. I'm free from it.

'So, am I going to be seeing Seb again sooner than I expected?' I ask, teasing him.

He blushes, something I haven't seen him do in a long time. 'Has it been that obvious that I like spending time with Seb's mum?' he says.

'Only a bit,' I reply jokingly. 'Does she like spending time with you too?'

He laughs. 'I don't know, we didn't talk about it.'

'Well you can't leave the country without telling her!'

Dad shrugs. 'We already said goodbye back in Wyoming,' he says. 'We live in different countries.'

'Who cares? You should tell her!' I urge. 'Grandma would tell you to. She'd say that life is short and that you should seize the day.'

He chews his bottom lip and checks his watch. 'I guess we have some time before our flight. They'll be at the hospital . . .'

'Yes!' I say, excited at the prospect of seeing Seb and his mum again.

After four more hours of driving and a switch to Cormac the Cadillac, we pull in to the hospital in Denver where Seb has been moved to.

'I hope this is the right place,' says Dad, looking nervous, as we wind through the corridors looking for Seb and his Mum.

Bandit is napping in my pocket, snoring gently.

We pass a mum and a tiny newborn. She's carrying a balloon that says it's a boy and cradling the baby in her arms. He clutches her finger with all of his.

I think of all the different versions of me. The one that wants to be like Grandma, the one that saved Seb in the wilderness, the one who goes to school back home. I finally feel like I can just be myself. And that's enough.

And if I have a few failures along the way, then that's OK. As Grandma would have said, it's better to try than not to do anything at all.

Seb

Denver, Colorado

7th July, 5 p.m.

♥ THE TEN OF HEARTS ♥

There's a surprise waiting for me at the hospital near home. Mom wheels me into a room. It's bright and warm with sun shining in. The walls and floor are white and clean. A screen covers the bed. The chest of drawers is full of cards and presents and notebooks and clothes.

I recognise the jacket hanging on the coatrack.

Mom pulls back the screen to the bed and there, sitting up and grinning at me, is Clay.

'CLAY!' I gasp, wheeling myself forwards in a rush. 'YOU'RE ALIVE!'

He has messy bed hair and is wearing a hospital gown. I grab his shoulders and hug him. He winces and I immediately ease off.

'Of course I'm alive,' he says.

'Are you going to be OK?' I ask. Waves of happiness wash over me.

'I'm not going to be OK. I am OK!' His eyes are wet and shiny. He looks small and different wired up to beeping machines, but when he smiles he's still the same Clay.

'Took you long enough to come and visit me,' says Clay jokingly.

'They wouldn't let me,' I reply quickly, just in case some part of Clay really believed I hadn't tried. '*All* I wanted was to come and see you.'

'I know,' he says. 'My dad told me.' His eyes glance over my bandaged leg. 'He didn't tell me about your leg though! What happened?'

And then there's a knock on the door and Vivi's dad enters followed by Vivi. I shake my head. 'What on earth are you doing here?'

'Josh?' says Mom.

'Can we have a quick moment outside?' Josh asks Mom. He looks a bit flustered and nervous. 'I don't have much time.'

They step outside together.

'Are you Clay?' asks Vivi, stepping forward.

'Wait, who's this?' Clay asks, frowning at me. 'How much did I miss?'

She smiles and holds out her hand. 'I'm Vivi. You tried to help my grandma in the gas station.'

Clay flinches and nods. 'I remember her. You have the same eyes.'

'I have loads to tell you,' I say.

'Be my guest . . .' says Clay, gesturing to the end of the bed.

I wheel myself closer to Clay and rest my bandaged leg on his bed. Vivi curls up in the chair. I start to tell Clay about our mission to the rainbow pool.

When we get to the part about the wolves, Clay interrupts and whispers, 'They say to look into the eyes of a wolf is to see your own soul.' Vivi and I glance at each other and smile.

After I've finished Clay looks between us, his eyes wide. 'Wow,' he says. 'That's better than any game I could have written.'

I grin back at him. I knew it would all be worth it.

'Did your deck of cards survive?' asks Clay.

I pull out the deck of cards. It's creased and covered in dried mud. Just then, Vivi's dad bursts into the room with Mom, carrying a fruit bowl and coffees. 'Here you go,' he says, handing out apples and bananas.

I smile at Mom and she comes over to give me a squeeze. 'I'm sorry I didn't tell you about Clay sooner,' she says, stroking my hair. 'I wanted it to be a surprise.'

'It's the best surprise ever,' I say.

I think of the wolf pack. Now it feels like we have our very own.

Somehow, Vivi and Clay have started talking about Pterodactyls. Soon they're both trying to convince me they *are* dinosaurs. I laugh, absent-mindedly shuffling my pack and picking a card.

The ten of hearts.

My favourite.

Hey Vivi,

You'll never guess what happened. I wrote a letter to apologise to the park rangers for not following the paths and to thank them for taking me to the hospital and they wrote back. They found the wolf pup! They fixed its leg and put a tracker collar on. Those wolves had recently formed their own pack and they're the most elusive in all of the park! Clay's better and Mr Evans brought in cupcakes for everyone for his first day back at school. My leg has almost fully healed too! Give Bandit a hug from me.

Love, Seb

Post Card

Hey Seb,

That's great! When it's our turn to visit, we should go back and find them. I wonder how big the pup will be? Guess what? Bandit did that thing where he plays dead again! Apparently it happens when ferrets are really tired.

Last week Dad dug out Grandma's diaries and it turned out she <u>did</u> fail an audition – loads in fact!

I know it's not quite Yellowstone, but I can't wait to show you where I live next month. You'll love the river and the canal. And you can watch me perform at the oldest theatre in town. I still can't believe they let me audition again. They invited me back after they found out what happened to Grandma. They'd already filled the part of Alice but guess which part they asked me to play? The Queen of Hearts. Dad will be happy to see you both too. I think he misses your mum.

Love, Vivi

Author Note

I first visited Colorado in 2014 and instantly fell in love with the Rocky Mountains. In 2019, when I was living in the States, I embarked on a trip of a lifetime: my husband and I packed up our trusty old car and drove 1,730 miles from Louisiana to Yellowstone National Park, stopping and camping in Colorado along the way. Being in the wilderness, watching chipmunks, moose and herds of bison, and hearing wolves howl at night made my heart sing. Often when I'm writing, it's the landscapes and settings that inspire the story and it was during this trip that the seeds of *Into the Volcano* were planted.

Whilst driving to Yellowstone, I had heard devastating news on the radio that there had been mass shootings in two different states, which sparked ideas for the event that would lead to Vivi and Seb being friends.

When we were in the park itself, we were very careful to follow the rules – maintaining a safe distance from animals and not stepping off any paths into the volcanic landscape — but my imagination was already running wild, wondering what it would be like to get lost somewhere like this.

I completed this book in 2020, a year that was filled with unknowns and anxieties for everyone due to the global pandemic. The mindfulness and breathing techniques that Seb uses in the story have come in handy for me many times. When I am anxious, I try and remember to stop and breathe, because no matter the darkness, there is always hope, kindness and wonder in the world, and for me I find it most when I'm in nature.

Acknowledgements

To Lena McCauley, who is not only an incredible editor but who I think possesses Seb's superpower of telepathy, because you know what I'm trying to say, even when I don't know how to say it myself. Thank you for all your brilliant ideas, enthusiasm, and making this book the best version of itself.

To my wonderful agent, Sallyanne Sweeney. I'm so grateful to be on this writing journey with you. Thank you for everything you do to make sure it continues. I can't wait to be eating cake with you in person again sometime soon.

Thank you to Genevieve Herr for copyediting the book as well as your valuable input, and to Ruth Girmatsion for taking the book through those important final stages.

To Rob Biddulph, I think this might be my favourite cover yet, although it's hard to choose because they're all so utterly gorgeous! Thank you. It's perfect.

To everyone at Hachette Children's. You're such a brilliant bunch and I'm privileged to work with you. Thank you for everything you do to create these books and get them into the hands of readers, with special thanks to publicity and marketing wonders Becci Mansell and Dom Kingston.

To my cousin, Ava Berry, and my sister, Olivia Butterworth. Without your help and support, I wouldn't have had the time, headspace or resources to write. I can't thank you enough.

To my amazing sister-in-law, Dr Emily Sandoz, for introducing me to Acceptance and Commitment Therapy and guiding my research.

To my cousin and actor extraordinaire, Ruby Wilde, for all your help with everything to do with drama and plays.

To my husband and fellow adventurer, Jonathan Kennison. There is lots of you and your wonderful family in this book. I feel especially privileged to have known Mawmaw deMahy. I thought about her often while writing this story.

To Jennifer Newbury, thank you for being my treasured workshop and writing partner.

To all the friends and family we stayed with on our road trip, especially Uncle Jimmy and Aunt Cathy, who showed me around Denver and Glenwood Springs, let us borrow their camping gear, and who told me the story of the mistaken use of bear spray. Also to my grandma-in-law, Betty Herrmann, and her family for hosting us in Amarillo, Texas, and to my friend, John Oliver, who we explored Yellowstone with and who took us walking in the Rocky Mountains armed with bear spray, and his aunt Jeanie for sharing her beautiful home in Jackson Hole, Wyoming. You all made our trip possible.

To my father-in-law, Rick Herrmann, for helping to organise our road trip route, your stories about growing up in Texas and answering my many questions about Cadillacs.

To my mother-in-law, Anne deMahy Herrmann, for all your continued support and explaining about school lockdowns and procedures in your capacity as school principal.

To the Natural History Museum for explaining everything I've ever wanted to know about dinosaurs!

To my friends and family, especially my mum, dad and sisters.

To teachers and librarians, thank you for promoting reading for pleasure and for all the spectacular work that you do.

To my readers, thank you so much! This book is for you.

Tash has to follow many rules to survive in Tibet, a
country occupied by Chinese soldiers. But when a man
sets himself on fire in protest and soldiers seize Tash's
parents, she and her best friend Sam must break the
rules. They are determined to escape Tibet – and seek the
help of the Dalai Lama himself in India.

And so, with a backpack of Tash's father's mysterious
papers and two trusty yaks by their side, their
extraordinary journey across the mountains begins.

Also by JESS BUTTERWORTH

When Ruby's dad uproots her from Australia to set up a hotel in the mountains of India, Ruby is devastated. Not only are they living in a run-down building in the middle of the wilderness, but Ruby is sure that India will never truly feel like home — not without her mum there.

Ever since her mum died, Ruby has been afraid. Of cars. Of the dark. Of going to sleep and never waking up. But then the last remaining leopards of the mountain are threatened and everything changes. Ruby vows to do all she can to protect them — if she can only overcome her fears . . .

Also by **JESS BUTTERWORTH**

Eliza and her sister Avery live in a small fishing village on the coast of Louisiana. But now, with sea levels rising, their home is at risk of being swept away.

Determined to save the land, Eliza and Avery secretly go searching in the swamp for the dangerous, wolf-like loup-garou. If they can prove this legendary creature exists, the government will have to protect its habitat — and their community.

But there's one problem: the loup-garou has never been seen before. And with a tropical storm approaching and the sisters deep in the swampland, soon it's not just their home at risk, but their lives as well . . .

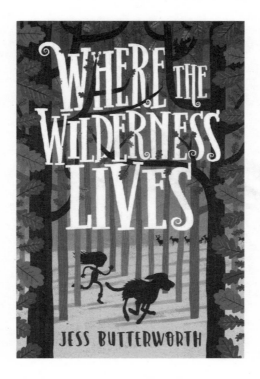

One day, as Cara and her siblings are trying to clean up the canal where they live, they pull out a mysterious locked safe. Though none of them can open it, they're sure it's something special.

That night, a thief comes after the safe. The children flee, travelling with their boat as far as they can, before continuing into the forest on foot. But soon they're lost in the mountains with a snowstorm about to land and food supplies running low.

Will Cara and her siblings be able to survive the wilderness with nothing but their wits, their bravery and one very large dog to help?